CHRONICLES OF THE MOON

LEGEND OF THE PHARAOH'S TOMB

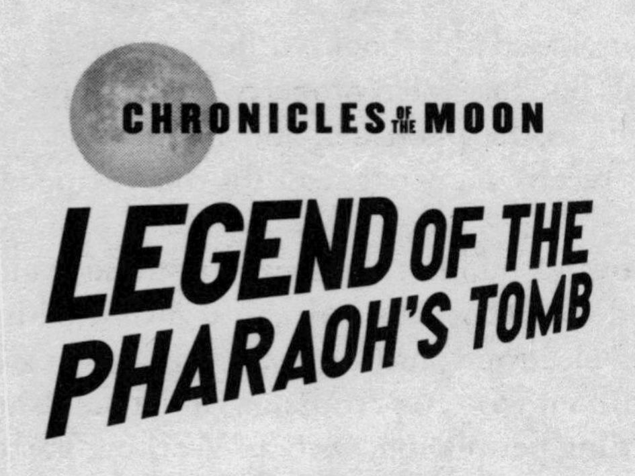

by Allan Frewin Jones

AN
APPLE
PAPERBACK

SCHOLASTIC INC

New York Toronto London Auckland Sydney
Mexico City New Delhi Hong Kong Buenos Aires

ISBN 0-439-80373-X

Created by Ben M. Baglio

12 11 10 9 8 7 6 5 4 3 2 5 6 7 8 9 10/0

Printed in the U.S.A. 40
First Scholastic printing, September 2005

CHRONICLES OF THE MOON

LEGEND OF THE PHARAOH'S TOMB

"Tremble in dread, thief and interloper: thou art revealed.
The Gods that protect these Halls know thy name,
Intruder in the resting place of Hathtut the Third,
Great King of Upper and Lower Egypt.
Thou hast brought down a curse upon thyself
That shall be visited upon thy family
Even unto the hundredth generation.
Thy first-born son shall die,
And so shall all the first-born sons of thy line,
Until the end of days."

The curse protecting the Funerary Text of
the Scroll of the Dead, found in the tomb of Hathtut III.
Translated by Lieutenant William Christie
of the 21st Light Dragoons, Luxor, August 1883.

PROLOGUE
Egypt, The Valley of the Kings
August 13, 1883

The barren valley was shrouded in the deep shadows of night. The sky was pierced with a thousand points of frozen white fire. And the ancient mountains lay awake, watching and waiting like monstrous, misshapen guardians.

All was silent. There was no wind. The entrance of the old tomb showed black in the cliffside — a deeper patch of darkness in the midnight shadows. It was known by the local people as the Pit of Ghosts.

Suddenly, a flurry of hoofbeats broke the stillness of the night. Three British cavalry officers galloped their horses down the long valley, shouting and laughing as they rode.

Twenty-year-old Lieutenant William Christie drew his horse to a halt outside the ancient tomb. His fellow officers had dared him to spend a night there and he had taken the challenge, throwing the dare back at them: "I'll ride to the Pit of Ghosts at midnight tonight! Who will come with me?"

Two had responded: Lieutenants George Cartwright and Charles Church, both the same age as William, both in high spirits and eager to defy the old legends of ghosts and curses.

The three men dismounted and secured their horses, wrapping the reins around large rocks to stop the animals from straying. Then they paused at the entrance to the tomb, while William struck a match and lit a rag-and-pitch torch. He smiled, amused to see his two companions holding back, waiting for him to make the first move.

A bleak, chill air struck his face as he stepped inside the tomb. The flame of the torch flickered, and for a moment William felt a strange uneasiness, but he shook it off and walked into the center of the chamber. "We'll build the fire here," he said, stamping his boot. His eyes gleamed. "I dare say the ghosts will be glad of the warmth and light." He let out a laugh that echoed within the stone walls. "Let's make ourselves at home."

George and Charles followed him in, carrying bundles of dry tinder. Soon the fire was lit and the three men sat on blankets, passing a flask and talking together in loud voices, their rowdy chatter awakening age-old echoes. The time slipped easily away as they laughed and joked together.

William took out his pocket watch. It was already

half past one. “The ghosts are boring company tonight,” he said, getting up to stretch his stiff legs.

“Maybe we scared them away,” Charles suggested with a smile.

“Ghosts!” shouted George. “You are neglecting your guests!”

All three men laughed.

William relit the torch and wandered the walls of the cavern. The faint remnants of old paintings were barely visible here and there on the stone. Even as a boy, he had been fascinated by artifacts and lost languages. With his posting to Egypt, William had seized the opportunity to explore the temple ruins and study the hieroglyphic texts of the ancient pharaohs.

He crouched to peer closely at a strange, hybrid creature — part crocodile, part leopard, and part hippopotamus — painted on a stone in the wall. Further investigation revealed that the stone, which was over a square foot in size, was loose, so William took out his pocketknife and dug at the edges. If he could pry it out, he could take it back to the barracks — absolute proof that he had won the dare. “Come over here and help me!” he called to his friends.

His companions joined him and they dug together at the crumbling edges of the stone.

"I can get my fingers around it," George said after a few minutes. "Stand back."

"I don't think so," William replied firmly. "The stone is mine."

"You're welcome to it," Charles told him. "I don't wish to be confronted by such an ugly sight every time I enter my quarters."

"Then you'd best avoid mirrors," William joked. He forced his fingers into the cracks, gripped the stone, and tugged until it came free, and he fell back clutching his prize.

"Look. There's a small chamber," said George, peering closely at the wall. "And something is inside."

William scrambled up. "Let me see."

The others made room for him. He held the torch close to the broken wall and the flickering light revealed an alcove cut into the stone. Within, a small clay jar lay on its side. It was about the size of a man's fist. William reached in and carefully drew it out.

The others gathered around him as he stared at the jar. There was a cartouche on the curved belly — the name of a pharaoh carved in hieroglyphics by some old scribe long ago. The jar had no lid, and the men could see that there was something rolled up inside.

"What is it?" Charles asked. "Is it worth anything?"

"Possibly," William replied. "It must be thousands of years old." He carried the jar over to the fire and leaned down to examine it in the firelight.

"If it's valuable, we will all benefit from it," said George.

Charles rubbed his hands together and held them out to the heat of the flames. "Fair shares for all," he said to William. "Will we be rich?"

"I have no idea," William answered thoughtfully. "Be quiet. I'm trying to read the writings."

George stretched out on his blanket, his arms behind his head. "Let the great scholar work," he said, smiling at Charles. "I will lie here and think of ways to spend my share of the profit."

William frowned, trying to remember the meanings of the ancient hieroglyphs.

"So?" George asked after a few moments. "What does it say?"

"Well . . ." William frowned. "One of the

symbols means *book*." He held the jar closer to the fire. "And there is another I recognize." He paused. "It's the symbol for *the dead*." A strange silence swallowed his words.

William looked up, feeling a sudden chill, as if an icy wind had swept through the chamber. On the other side of the fire, George sat up and he and Charles stared at William through flames that flickered as yellow as poison.

William gazed back at his companions uneasily. He felt horribly cold and moved closer to the fire, noticing that his friends were also drawing in, their faces bleak and their hands reaching forward for warmth. William stretched his fingers almost into the fire. But there was no heat. The flames were cold. He snatched his hand back, startled and alarmed.

He thought he heard voices — whispering voices — coming from the direction of the small alcove. He turned his head to stare at the dark hole, his eyes wide with alarm.

"God preserve us!" Charles murmured. They could all hear the voices now. They could all see the threads of blackness that oozed from the opening and crawled across the sandy floor. The eerie voices grew louder — an incomprehensible babble of anger and menace.

All three men moved at once, scrambling to their feet, backing away from the sinister opening. William glanced at his companions. He saw their faces distorted with fear and felt a cold sweat running down his own face.

The ghastly chorus rose. William thought it sounded like a thousand dead men giving voice to an undying rage. Mesmerized, he watched the crawling blackness reach the fire and snuff it out.

Then, tearing himself away, he snatched up his gear and threw himself toward the cavern entrance. His friends were close at his heels, fighting one another to be free of the tomb.

"The jar is yours!" George shouted to William. "I want nothing to do with it — or with this vile place!"

"Neither do I!" Charles put in, as he reached for his horse. "I beg you to leave it!"

Once outside, they found that the horses were whinnying and straining at the reins, their eyes wide and rolling in fear. Wordlessly, the soldiers mounted up and rode, galloping, away from the Pit of Ghosts.

Vengeful voices shrieked on the wind that howled in the riders' wake.

And then there was no wind. The icy stars stared

down. The mountains watched and waited in the silence of the night.

~~~~~

William sat in his barracks in Luxor. The fear that had sent him and his friends galloping from the tomb had melted away on their return to town. William had ignored his companions' appeals to join them in some crowded backstreet restaurant and waste the rest of the night away. He had work to do. He wanted to learn the secrets of the ancient jar.

An oil lamp cast a pool of light onto his desk. The empty jar stood to one side. It had contained a thick roll of papyrus pages, which William had carefully withdrawn and smoothed out upon the desktop. They were covered with ancient writings.

Slowly he had written out a translation of the first page on a sheet of white paper, consulting textbooks when his memory failed him. Now, at last, the translation was complete.

The Book of Passage Through the Halls of the Dead. William stared down at the extraordinary words that he had scribbled on the notepaper.

Away beyond the sharp-edged hills, the sun was rising, but William was too absorbed in his work to notice. From what William had translated thus far,
~~~~~

he knew the papyrus pages contained a sacred text, buried with the dead pharaoh. The pages were meant to guide the pharaoh's immortal soul into the afterlife. So essential was this text that a curse had been placed upon it, so that no one would dare remove it from the tomb.

Thou hast brought down a curse upon thyself that shall be visited upon thy family even unto the hundredth generation. Thy firstborn son shall die, and so shall all the firstborn sons of thy line, until the end of days, William read. Uneasiness crept into his mind. It was a terrible curse.

William wrestled with his fears. His rational mind told him that this was just the superstition of a long-dead people — uncanny, but powerless. But the terror that had consumed him in the tomb came creeping back, and his hand trembled as he held the sheet of white paper to the flame of his oil lamp and watched it burn.

He stood up, walked to the door, and threw it open. The pale blue sky outside was streaked with the amber light of dawn. A trumpet rang out, sounding reveille to rouse the soldiers and, with it, William's fear drained away. "Feebleminded superstition," he whispered to himself. "The curse means nothing!"

Quickly, he returned to his desk, rolled up the papyrus text and pushed it back inside the jar. Then he stashed the jar at the bottom of his footlocker, slammed the lid shut, and turned to face another hot Egyptian day.

Chapter One: The Elephantine Stone

The Valley of the Kings, Egypt
Present Day

The bright sun shone down into the valley, bleaching the hills and beating down upon the bustle and chaos of the great archaeological excavation. Jeeps bounced along dirt tracks, sending up plumes of dust. The slopes of the hills crawled with men in white galabia robes, wielding picks and shovels or carrying baskets of rubble up and down the steep inclines. Donkeys moved surefootedly among the stones, carrying supplies for the broad encampment of tents and trailers. Everywhere, there was noise — of metal striking stone, voices speaking in English and Arabic, and engines struggling in the heat. They were the sounds of the work that uncovered ancient history.

A line of local men were carrying baskets of earth away from a recently opened tomb, cut deep into the hillside. The tomb had been carved into the cliffs at the far end of the western arm of the valley, some distance from the site of most of the royal burials. Inside, the air was still and cool, and a cable snaked along the sloping corridor, powering bright electric lights.

Four people stood in the tomb: twelve-year-old Olivia Christie and her best friend, Josh Welles — just two weeks her junior — along with Olivia's father, Professor Kenneth Christie of Oxford University, and his assistant, Jonathan Welles, Josh's twenty-four-year-old brother. The two men were stooping to peer at some wall carvings.

"Be careful, Josh." Olivia Christie's blue eyes sparkled in the lamplight. "There might be booby traps." She was tall and slim, with long, dark hair and a pale, inquisitive face. Her British accent added a tone of formality even to her jokes.

Josh Welles paused for a moment. From under his blond, shaggy bangs he peered down the long sloping passageway of ancient limestone. He pushed his hair out of his eyes. "Nice try, Olly!" he said. "But I know the tombs around here weren't booby-trapped." He called out to the two men. "It was the pyramids that had all the traps to catch grave robbers, wasn't it? There aren't any here, are there?"

The professor and his assistant were closely scrutinizing a section of the tomb wall that was carved with hieroglyphics. The professor seemed not to hear, but Jonathan turned his head and smiled at his younger brother's question. He had the same warm brown eyes as Josh, and the same shaggy thatch of blond hair.

"Normally, you'd be right," Jonathan said. "But Setiankhra was a pharaoh with a big secret. And a great treasure. He wasn't prepared to rely entirely on the remoteness of the valley and the Necropolis Guards to defend that secret against intruders — so he had the tomb builders add some nasty little devices of his own."

Olly looked at him. "How nasty?" she asked nervously. Her comment to Josh about booby traps had been a joke — or so she had thought. She stared down at the stones beneath her feet. They looked solid enough, but she was beginning to regret her eagerness to come on the guided tour of the recently excavated tomb.

"Come with me and I'll show you some of them," Jonathan offered. He looked at the professor. "Is that OK with you, Professor?"

Kenneth Christie looked up. "What's that?" He had been so caught up in his deciphering that he hadn't heard a word. Olly adored her father, with his untidy graying hair, disheveled clothes, and half-moon glasses on a cord around his neck, but she did find it a little frustrating when he went off into a world of his own and didn't hear a thing that was said to him.

Jonathan repeated the question.

"Yes, that'll be fine," the professor said absent-mindedly, already turning back to the wall. "Some of these writings are very intriguing," he murmured. "Third Kingdom — definitely."

Jonathan led Olly and Josh down to a place where the passageway leveled out. Olly guessed that they must now be at least thirty feet under the towering cliffs of the desolate valley. It was an awesome thought.

The walls and ceilings of the passageway were covered in intricate designs — columns of hieroglyphic script and drawings of strange and fabulous beast-men with snake-heads and bird-heads and dog-heads. Jonathan shined his flashlight at a particular section of the wall. It was pocked with a series of holes. Josh and Olly stepped closer to look. In the lamplight they could see that each of the holes was blocked by something deep inside — something slender and sharp.

"Those are stone spikes," Jonathan explained. "If a robber triggered the trap, they'd shoot out and impale him. Straight through the gut."

"Wow!" breathed Olly, wide-eyed. "Are they safe?"

"Of course they are," Josh said. "Jonathan and your dad wouldn't let us down here if we were likely to get stone spikes through our heads." He looked at his brother, his voice a little uneasy. "That's right, isn't it?"

Jonathan nodded. "Exactly right," he agreed.

The professor came up behind them. "Impalement was the preferred method of execution for tomb robbers," he said. "To break into a tomb and steal the grave goods was the worst crime imaginable." He frowned, shaking his head. "But someone managed to get in here without falling foul of the booby traps. This tomb was looted a long time ago — probably within a few centuries of its being sealed."

Olly looked at her father. "How would the spikes have been triggered?" she asked curiously.

"I imagine it would have been a mechanism involving wires and pulleys and counterbalances," replied the professor. "It's possible that they wouldn't still work after thousands of years" — he pointed across the floor — "but these stones were placed with great precision," he explained, "balanced to tilt at the pressure of a foot and hurl the unwary intruder into a deep pit."

Olly's eyes widened. She noticed that tapered blocks of wood had been hammered into cracks between the stones.

"Don't worry," her father assured her. "It's quite safe as long as no one removes the wedges."

"But it wasn't just spikes and pits," Jonathan added. "There were enormous stones that would drop from the roof to crush intruders, and poison smeared on door handles, and pitchers of toxic powder carefully positioned to fall and break when a door was opened — not to mention wires stretched across the corridors at neck height, ready to cut a robber's head off."

Josh and Olly exchanged nervous glances.

"They had some pretty unpleasant ways of dealing with burglars back then," Olly remarked.

"They certainly did." Professor Christie had come to the end of the lights powered by the cable from the electric generator. He unclipped a flashlight from his belt and switched it on. The bright beam revealed a second long slope, which he began to descend.

"Professor, I'm going up top for a few minutes," Jonathan said. "I've seen a few things near the entrance that I'd like to check on." He turned and headed up the passage to the small square of daylight that marked the mouth of the tomb.

Josh and Olly looked at each other.

"Do you think they found *all* the traps?" Josh said.

"I hope so," Olly replied. She switched on a flashlight of her own and hurried down the corridor to catch up with her father.

Josh followed. "All the same — you won't *touch* anything, will you?" he said to her. "You know what you're like."

Olly glanced at him, eyebrows raised. "Meaning?"

"Meaning don't go poking around without asking your dad first," he answered firmly. "I don't want to get squashed flat by a great big stone because you've accidentally set off some old booby trap."

"I'm not a complete idiot," Olly said with a laugh. "I won't touch a thing. I promise."

Josh smiled. "Good."

Even though Olly had a talent for being impulsive and often looking before she leaped, she didn't need Josh to tell her to be cautious. The tomb had only been discovered four weeks ago. And it was very big, with at least eighteen chambers. Hardly anything was known yet about the breathtaking, three-and-a-half-thousand-year-old burial site, apart from the fact that it had once housed the mummy of a pharaoh named Setiankhra.

Professor Christie had discovered its location after translating hieroglyphic carvings on a stone he had found on Elephantine — an island in the Nile, known locally as Abu. Immediately after deciphering the stone, the professor had postponed the group's return to England and arranged for them to oversee the excavation of the tomb.

Olly had been on several expeditions with Josh, Jonathan, and her father, but she had rarely seen the professor as excited as when he had found this artifact. They now referred to the priceless object as the Elephantine Stone. Even though it was no bigger than a man's fist, the writings on the stone held great meaning. They had not only given directions to the lost tomb of Pharaoh Setiankhra, they had also referred to something even more astonishing. The writings indicated that within the tomb lay hidden one of the Talismans of the Moon!

This was astonishing because the Talismans of the Moon were the stuff of legend — of film and fantasy. Olly never tired of hearing Jonathan and her father discuss the incredible story attached to them. According to the legend, the Talismans of the Moon had been created in ancient times by priests from different cultures around the world — priests who all served the moon god, or goddess, of their people. Each of these priests crafted a single talisman. And it was said that if all these talismans were brought together, in the right place, then a great secret of knowledge, learning, and time would be revealed.

So went the legend, but the writings on the Elephantine Stone were the first indication that the myth *might* have some basis in reality.

From his research through ancient Egyptian, Assyrian, Greek and Roman texts, Professor Christie had come to believe that the Talismans of the Moon were in fact the key to unlocking the lost Archive of the Old. The Archive was thought to be a structure that contained ancient and secret records of lost civilizations. The Archive of the Old was also the stuff of legend — a legend that the professor had long believed to be true. If the talismans really opened the Archive, then they could indeed be said to reveal a great secret of knowledge, learning, and time — for the Archive of the Old supposedly contained a copy of every magical text of its era.

Since concluding that the Archive really did exist — somewhere — Professor Christie had made it his life's work to find it. And so the possibility that the Talismans of the Moon might *also* exist had filled him with excitement and had brought him — as well as Olly, Josh, and Jonathan — here to Setiankhra's tomb in the Valley of the Kings. Somehow, buried in all this sand, one of the four Talismans of the Moon might truly exist.

Josh and Olly walked gingerly across the wedged, booby-trapped stones and followed the professor down the second corridor. Shadowy chambers opened on either side, and Olly glimpsed stunning paintings and carvings within them.

The professor paused, pointing the flashlight toward an odd, circular painting. "That is a picture of the snake that devours itself," he said. "It's an ancient symbol of eternity. And around it are the seven stars that the Egyptians called the Krittikas — the Judges of Mankind. We know them as the Pleiades."

"Imagine how much work it took to get all this done," Olly murmured in amazement.

"And then they just sealed up the whole thing and forgot about it," Josh put in.

"Yes, indeed," the professor said. "Scores of workers toiled down here, using only wooden clubs and copper chisels. They labored day after day for ten years or more. And their only light came from small, flickering oil lamps." He paused at the entrance to another chamber, shining the flashlight beam from side to side. To the left it revealed a life-sized statue of a jackal-headed man with evil, gleaming green eyes.

"Yikes!" Olly exclaimed, startled by the malevolence in the painted eyes. "Who's he?"

"A shabti warrior," her father told her. "The writings here are spells and incantations intended to bring the pharaoh's magical guardians to life, should anyone attempt to break the great seal and enter his Burial Chamber."

"So this warrior could jump off the wall and come to life? Who'd believe that?" Josh queried lightly.

The professor turned and looked at him. "Never dismiss things simply because you don't understand them, Josh," he said. He moved the flashlight beam over the square entrance way. "Not everything can be scientifically explained."

Olly turned her flashlight to Josh and saw him staring at her father, looking puzzled. Then she shined the light on the shabti warrior and his chamber. The doors stood wide open and the floor was silted and strewn with debris.

"This is the result of flooding," observed Professor Christie. "Every few hundred years this region suffers torrential rainstorms. Millions of tons of floodwater pour into the valley, even seeping into the tombs themselves." He sighed. "It's caused immense damage."

"Is one of those storms due any time soon?" Olly asked. "If I'd known I'd have brought an umbrella." She looked back up the narrow way they had come, imagining a murderous flood of black water roaring down to engulf them.

"I think the meteorologists would have warned us," her father replied, not really acknowledging his daughter's attempt at humor.

"Excuse me," Josh asked, "but if this is the Burial Chamber, where's the sarcophagus?" He knew that the mummified body of the pharaoh, in its gold-encrusted casket, was usually placed within a great hollowed-out stone box — but there was no such box in the chamber. The chamber was empty.

"That's a very good question," Professor Christie replied. "It ought to be in here, but it clearly isn't."

"Maybe the robbers took it?" Olly suggested.

"No, the sarcophagus would have been made of granite or quartzite," her father responded, "and the robbers were searching for gold." He stepped into the room, shining his flashlight on the lavishly decorated walls. "I suspect that there's a hidden doorway." He walked across the uneven floor and stooped to examine some writings. "There must be a clue here somewhere," they heard him mutter.

"When my dad finds the secret door and the treasures, he'll be famous!" Olly told Josh delightedly. "Hey, Dad! I bet there'll be TV shows about you. And books and computer games — maybe even a Hollywood movie!"

Professor Christie stared at her. "I hope not," he replied. "I'd never get any work done with all that kind of nonsense going on."

"No problem," Olly assured him. "I'll do the TV shows for you."

Her father smiled indulgently. "I think you're getting a little ahead of yourself, Olivia," he said. "So far, all I have are riddles and puzzles. It could take years of painstaking research before the secrets of Setiankhra's tomb reveal themselves — if they ever do."

"Of course they will," Olly declared with absolute conviction. "You're a genius, Dad. You'll solve the mystery."

Her father laughed gently and turned to study the cryptic wall paintings again. "Just like her mother," Olly and Josh heard him say fondly.

It was several years since Olly's mother had died in a plane crash during an expedition to Papua New Guinea. Since then, Olly's grandmother had accompanied the father and daughter all over the world, overseeing the domestic arrangements and acting as a stern but affectionate tutor for Olly and Josh.

Josh and Jonathan's mother, Natasha Welles, was a film star. She spent so much time filming in foreign locations, she was often away from home for long periods of time. That was why Josh traveled with his older brother on archaeological expeditions. Besides, Olly's gran also thought it was good for Olly to have someone her own age around.

Olly looked at her friend. "Wouldn't it be great if the two of *us* found the secret doorway?" she said. "I mean, there are only so many walls in here. How difficult can it be?"

Josh looked at her dubiously. "Pretty difficult, I bet," he replied. "Besides, it may not even be in here. It might be in one of those other rooms we saw on the way down. If I were hiding something, I wouldn't hide it in the most obvious room in the whole tomb. I'd be sneakier than that."

Olly looked at him. "You know, that's not a bad idea," she said. Josh was always practical. Sometimes it was frustrating, but she had to admit that it could be helpful, too. She shouted to her father, "Is it OK if we explore some of the other rooms?"

"As long as you're careful," her father called back. "Very careful."

Olly led the way, raking the floor with her flashlight as they headed back up the corridor. They reached a small, square chamber. Paintings and writings covered the walls, some still bright and well-preserved, others smeared and stained and fragmented. Olly pointed her flashlight into the dark corners. Silt was piled against the wall — testament to the ancient floods.

"We should do this scientifically," Josh said. He pointed. "Let's start over there and work our way around. We need to look for regular cracks, and parts of the walls that are sunken or that stick out more than the rest."

They began to pick their way across the debris left by three thousand years of floodwater. The beam of the flashlight lit up a stylized painting of a jackal-headed being.

"He looks like that shabti warrior," Josh said. He glanced at Olly. "What did your father mean about not dismissing stuff just because you don't understand it? Was he talking about the magic spells?" He gave a crooked grin. "He doesn't think they might work, does he?"

Olly's eyes gleamed in the flashlight beam. "You wouldn't think so, but my family is kind of weird," she replied.

Josh laughed. "Tell me about it."

She shook her head. "No, I mean *really* weird."

Josh stared at her expectantly.

"I'm not saying *I* necessarily believe this, all right?" she continued. "But there's a possibility — just a possibility — that there's a curse on my family."

Josh opened his mouth to laugh, but the look in Olly's eyes silenced him. "Are you kidding me?" he breathed. "A curse? Really? That's so cool. What's the story?"

"Well, they say it dates back to the end of the nineteenth century," Olly began solemnly. "It's all the fault of my great-great-grandfather, William Christie."

Josh listened in amazement as Olly told him how William had removed a sacred scroll from an old tomb and then made a translation of the curse.

"So, what happened next?" Josh asked. "Did he die in some weird way?"

"No, *he* didn't die," Olly replied. "That wasn't the curse. His firstborn son, Edmund, was the one who died . . . of tuberculosis in 1907. He was seventeen."

"But that wasn't all that strange back in those days," Josh pointed out. "People died of nasty diseases all the time."

"I haven't finished," Olly said. "William had a second son named Frances. Well, William died in 1939. While Frances and *his* son, Adam — his *firstborn* son — were going through William's things, they found his diaries and this old pot with papyrus pages in it. Frances and Adam read the diaries and learned that the papyrus pages were an ancient text that included a curse on all of the firstborn sons in the family. They also read that William had forgotten all about the curse till his first son died. Then he began to wonder if it was the curse that had killed Edmund."

Josh looked doubtfully at Olly. "And now you're not going to tell me that Adam died, too, are you?"

"You bet I am," responded Olly. She was about to continue, when a strange booming sound interrupted her. It echoed around the tomb, coming from outside the room, further up the passageway. Josh and Olly looked at each other, puzzled by the noise. It was a few moments before they realized that they were hearing the distorted sound of a human voice. Someone was shouting in alarm.

The voice drew closer, and a figure ran past the chamber they were in. Olly was shocked to realize that it was Jonathan. Wondering what possibly could have happened, she and Josh ran after him as he burst into the lower chamber where Professor Christie was working.

"What's all this noise?" the professor exclaimed. "I can't hear myself think!"

"Professor! It's gone!" Jonathan Welles gasped.

The professor and the two friends stared at him.

"What's gone?" Professor Christie asked.

"The stone!" Jonathan cried. "Someone has stolen the Elephantine Stone!"

Chapter Two: Thief!

The city of Luxor lies several miles from the remote, tomb-pocked Valley of the Kings. Two police officers came from there in response to Jonathan Welles's telephone call. Polite and efficient, they examined the trailer from which the Elephantine Stone had been stolen, making notes and asking questions in fluent English.

The small trailer seemed very crowded. Olly and Josh were there, along with the professor, and Olly's grandmother, Audrey Beckmann, who acted as Olly and Josh's tutor while they were on expedition. Audrey sat between the two youngsters, her sharp, intelligent eyes taking everything in. Her gray hair was cut into a short, smart bob. She wore a crisp white blouse, khaki trousers, and stylish but practical suede boots.

There was an air of gloom in the trailer as Professor Christie explained to the police officers the importance of the lost stone. "It is an artifact of immeasurable value," he told them. "Please do everything you can to find the thief and retrieve the stone."

The officer in charge looked at a photograph that had been taken shortly after the Elephantine Stone's discovery. "It is a shame the safe was so easily broken into. Artifacts such as this command very high prices," he said. "It is possible that the stone is already on its way to the illegal markets in Cairo." He saw the look of despair on the professor's face. "But do not fear, Professor Christie, we will ask many questions of many people. *Inshallah* — God willing — we will find the stone and return it to you." The police officers stepped down from the trailer.

"I can't believe it!" Olly wailed. "We were down in the tomb talking about robbers from thousands of years ago, and at the same time someone was up here making off with the Elephantine Stone!"

"At least we've still got photos, and copies of the writings on the stone," Josh pointed out. "It's not like we all have to give up and go home. We can still follow its clues to the talisman."

Jonathan frowned at him. "That's not the point, Josh," he sighed. Olly could understand his frustration. Her father wasn't blaming him, but she knew he must feel responsible for the loss. The safe had been located in his trailer.

Professor Christie lifted his hand. “No, Josh is right,” he said. “We must continue our work and allow the police to do theirs.”

Audrey Beckmann stood up. “There’s obviously nothing more we can do,” she said. She looked at Josh and Olly. “You two need to wash that dirt off your hands and come over to my trailer for your lessons.”

Olly looked up at her gran in surprise. “I won’t be able to concentrate on lessons with all this going on,” she said.

Audrey Beckmann frowned. “Oh, I think I’ll be able to help you concentrate,” she said. “You know the rules, Olly: three hours of class a day during the school year.” She headed for the door. “I’ll expect to see the two of you in five minutes — with your math books.”

The door closed sharply behind her.

Olly looked appealingly at her father. “Maybe we could help look for the stone,” she said. “I’ve been thinking, and . . .”

Professor Christie stared at her in alarm. “No, Olivia,” he said firmly. “We’ll leave the investigation to the police.” He turned to Jonathan. “We shouldn’t dwell on this,” he said. “There’s still plenty of work to be done. I’ve found some interesting inscriptions in the Burial Chamber. I'd like you to come and look at them with me. And bring the translation of the stone — I think it will be useful."

Olly and Josh left the trailer.

Josh looked at his friend. "So, *what* have you been thinking?" he asked.

"I've got a theory," Olly said, her bright eyes gleaming. "The thief must have kept watch on the trailer, and sneaked in the moment Jonathan's back was turned, right?" She looked at Josh. "Which means it has to be someone who works here — maybe one of the diggers."

Josh nodded. "And *that* means the stone is probably still here," he said excitedly. "Hidden away till the end of the day."

"Exactly," Olly agreed. "So as soon as Gran finishes with us, I propose we search high and low for the stone."

"Sounds like the fastest way to get it back to me." Josh grinned. "Can you imagine the look on Jonathan's face when we hand the stone back to him? It'll be great!"

They stopped to wash their grimy hands and pick up their school books before heading over to Audrey's trailer.

"So, what happened to Adam anyway?" Josh asked curiously. Olly had interrupted the tale of her family curse when Jonathan had announced the theft, and Josh was eager to hear the end — in spite of all that had just happened.

Olly stared at him, her mind still full of plans for finding the Elephantine Stone. "Huh? Oh — how could I forget? Yes, Great-Uncle Adam. He was my grandfather's older brother," Olly explained. "Well, apparently, when he read about the curse, he got really nervous — like you would if you believed in curses and you were the firstborn son who was going to die! His father tried to convince him that the curse couldn't possibly be real, but Adam was totally spooked. He thought he could end the whole curse thing by taking the sacred papyrus text to Egypt and putting it back in the tomb it came from." Olly shook her head. "Big mistake."

"He died?" Josh asked.

"His ship was hit by a really big storm and sank without trace," Olly told him. "Great-Uncle Adam — and the pot and the sacred text and everything — went down with the ship." She looked solemnly at Josh. "The curse had claimed its second victim."

Josh frowned. "But Adam only died because he believed in the curse," he said. "Otherwise, he wouldn't have been on that ship in the first place. That's exactly how these curse things work. You tell someone they're cursed, and then the curse comes true. But only because they *believe* in it."

Olly sighed. "Uncle Douglas didn't believe in it. And it got him, too," she said.

Josh stared. "Who's Uncle Douglas?"

They had almost reached the trailer now. The door was opened from inside and Olly's grandmother appeared in the doorway. "Come along, you two," she called. "You won't learn anything by wasting time out there." She withdrew, leaving the door open for them.

"What about Uncle Douglas?" Josh hissed urgently to Olly.

"Later," Olly whispered back. "Don't mention him in front of Gran. She doesn't like talking about it."

^^^^^

It was late in the afternoon when Olly and Josh finally escaped the watchful eye of Audrey Beckmann, and Josh was eager to hear the rest of Olly's family history. "So, how did your Uncle Douglas die?" he asked her.

"He was killed in a car crash in 1964," she replied. "He was nineteen. He was my dad's older brother — my grandfather's firstborn son. Dad was born next, then Aunt Anna."

Josh was quiet for a few moments as he took this in. "Why did you tell me not to mention him in front of your grandma?" he asked at length. "She's your *mother's* mother, isn't she? She wasn't directly related to your dead uncle. Why would it bother her?"

Olly shrugged. "Gran just doesn't like anyone talking about the curse. We never mention it in front of her."

"I get it," Josh said. "She thinks the curse is a load of rubbish?"

"That's what Dad says," Olly responded. "But if you ask me, I think it's the other way around. I think she's afraid that the curse is *real*. That's why she won't talk about it."

Josh stared at her. The idea that Olly's level-headed gran might actually believe in the curse was the most alarming thing that he had heard so far. "What does your dad think about all this?" he asked.

Olly frowned. "It's difficult to tell," she said. "He acts like it's all mumbo jumbo, but the reason he got into archaeology in the first place was because of the curse. He did tons of research — following the curse back and checking it out in the archives and so on. And here's the thing: He found some old inscriptions in the British Museum that said that copies of all the old sacred texts, from all the tombs, were kept in the The Archive of the Old." She looked at her friend. "So, you have to ask yourself: Is Dad searching for the Talismans of the Moon because he wants to open the Archive for academic purposes? Or is he doing it so that he can find a copy of the text that William Christie took from Hathtut's tomb, and put it back — like Great-Uncle Adam was trying to do — and end the curse?"

"Wow!" breathed Josh. "You weren't kidding when you said your family is weird."

Olly gave a faint smile. She didn't tell him about what sometimes kept her awake at night. The curse only mentioned the death of firstborn *sons*. But what would happen if no boys were born? Her Aunt Anna had no children, so Olly was the only one in her entire family. Would the lack of boys break the curse? Or would it switch to the firstborn daughter, instead? Olly was a very headstrong girl, and she wondered: If a girl could do anything that boys can do, did that include being plagued by a family curse?

The searing heat of the day had lessened, but the canyon was still as hot as an oven as the two friends walked over to where the diggers were working. Olly looked out across the site. There was no sign of Jonathan or her father. She assumed they were down in the tomb. The laborers were being supervised by Mohammed, a handsome young Egyptian who had been hired for his knowledge of the valley and its history. He was a student of Egyptology from Cairo University, and he spoke fluent English. Olly liked him. He was always polite and courteous, although he was quick to bark orders at anyone who wasn't working hard enough.

"So, where do we start our search for the stone?" Josh asked. "We can't exactly go through everyone's pockets."

Olly looked around thoughtfully. There was a tent nearby where much-needed bottled drinking water was kept. Many of the diggers kept small bundles of possessions there, too, heaped together out of the direct sunlight. "If you keep watch for me," Olly suggested, "I can go into that tent and quickly look through the packs."

Josh's forehead wrinkled. "Are you sure that's a good idea?" he asked.

Olly frowned. "Well, I wouldn't do it under normal circumstances," she admitted. "But we do want to find the Elephantine Stone, don't we?"

"We do."

"And it's not like I'll be prying," Olly continued, "because I'll just feel the packs, and if I come across anything that feels like the stone, then I'll look more closely. That's OK, isn't it?"

"I guess so," Josh said, still feeling uneasy. He shrugged. "Well, this is really important. OK. I'll keep watch — but be quick."

Olly nodded, and with a final nervous glance at the workers, she turned and slipped into the tent.

To her dismay, she found Jonathan standing there, a bottle of water in his hand and a very unhappy look on his face.

"Get in here, Josh," he ordered.

Josh slunk in and stood at Olly's side.

"I can't believe what I just heard," Jonathan said. "You can't just go through people's private possessions! What were you thinking?"

"We want to help find the stone," Olly explained. "We thought it might still be on site."

"You can help by keeping out of the way," Jonathan told her firmly. His eyes moved from Olly to Josh and then back to Olly. "No more bright ideas, OK?"

Olly nodded. "OK," she muttered.

Jonathan herded them out of the tent and went to speak to Mohammed, leaving Olly and Josh rather crestfallen.

"That was terrible," Olly groaned. "Maybe trying to find the stone isn't such a good idea after all." Olly was surprised when Josh shook his head.

"We can't give up yet," he said. "Listen, I have an idea. Why don't we go over to the canteen and have a word with Ahmed? He might know something."

Olly's face brightened. "That's an excellent plan," she said. "We could ask him a few casual questions about the diggers. He knows everything that goes on here. He'll be able to tell us if anyone has been acting suspiciously. Good idea, Josh!"

~~~

The canteen was a large wooden shack at the southern end of the site. It was run by Ahmed Farfour, a beefy, bald-headed man who acted as cook, waiter, and source of all news, gossip, and information for the entire valley. Ahmed had the radio on. It was playing traditional Saidi music, with
~~~

its reedy swirls of notes and its strong, hypnotic rhythms.

The two friends preferred to go into the canteen through the back entrance. That way they ended up right next to the counter — among Ahmed's tempting snacks. Olly was a particular fan of the thick, syrupy pastries, and the freshly squeezed orange juice, sweetened with sugarcane. Josh liked the freshly baked pita bread and the dipping sauces: hummus, baba ganoush, and spicy tahini.

The back door was ajar when they arrived. Olly stopped so suddenly that Josh almost walked into her. Before he could speak, Olly gestured to him to keep quiet.

Through the narrow crack in the door, Josh heard Ahmed's voice. He was speaking in heavily accented English. At first Josh thought he was talking to someone in the canteen, but after a moment he realized that Ahmed was speaking on a cell phone.

"I cannot get away yet," Ahmed was saying, his voice an urgent, hushed growl. "No, not today. It is impossible. Tell him I will meet him at the market in Luxor at the stall of Khaled the spice merchant. Yes, that's the place. Tell him to be there early — soon after dawn. And tell him that if we can come to an agreement, it will prove profitable for us both. Speak of this to no one else."

The two friends stared at one another. Josh gestured to Olly and they crept away from the building. "What do you think he was talking about?" Olly asked. "It sounded very suspicious to me."

Josh nodded. "Well, if I had to guess, I'd say that Ahmed stole the Elephantine Stone," he whispered. "It sounded like he was arranging to hand it over to someone."

"Amazing!" Olly breathed. "Case solved. We have to tell Dad and Jonathan."

She turned to go, but Josh caught her arm. "I don't think that's such a great idea right now," he hissed. "Ahmed has probably hidden the stone. What if he convinces them that what we heard was totally innocent? They'll go nuts — especially after what Jonathan just said."

"You're right," Olly said thoughtfully. Then suddenly her eyes lit up. "This means we'll have to go to Luxor first thing tomorrow morning, hide near the spice merchant's stall, and catch Ahmed red-handed, selling the stone!"

Josh thought about this. There seemed to him to be a major flaw in Olly's plan. "How are we going to get there?" he asked. "It's four miles away on the other side of the river, and we can't exactly ask Jonathan or your dad to drive us over there at that time of day."

Olly frowned. "Good point," she said. But then she smiled. "Got it! You get along with Abdullah, and *he* looks after the donkeys. Do you think you could persuade him to lend us a couple?"

"He'll want something in exchange," Josh said. "I'll have to think about what we could give him." He glanced at Olly. "You know, we'll need to get up pretty early to be in Luxor by dawn."

Olly groaned. "I'll never wake up in time." They both knew Olly was not a morning person.

"Don't worry, I've got an alarm on my watch," Josh told her, grinning. "I'll make sure you're awake."

Olly frowned at him. "Just wake me gently," she said. "Otherwise I'll be in a terrible mood all morning, and you won't like that at all." And with that she turned and walked off to her trailer.

Josh gazed after her with a quiet smile, wondering what was going to be more dangerous: spying on Ahmed, or waking Olly up in the middle of the night.

Chapter Three: The Souk at Luxor

The Valley of the Kings was shrouded in darkness as Josh and Olly made their stealthy way toward the donkey pen at the far eastern end of the archaeological dig. Behind a wicker fence, the animals stood quiet and still in the gray gloom. Abdullah, the donkey boy, lay sleeping in his hut, his head pillowed on two comic books that Josh had traded for the loan of two donkeys.

"Which are ours?" Olly whispered, leaning over the fence and patting the nearest donkey. It nuzzled her hand, sniffing for food. "Sorry, donkey — I don't have anything for you," she murmured fondly.

"Abdullah said to take any of them," Josh replied.

A few minutes later, they led two donkeys out of the pen. It took Olly several attempts to mount up — the donkey kept moving every time she tried to climb on board. Josh sat astride his own docile animal, watching and grinning at her efforts.

"This is hard work," Olly puffed, finally getting herself in place on the donkey's back. She pulled the reins and gave the donkey a tap on both sides with her heels. "C'mon, boy," she said. "Let's go!" The donkey didn't move.

Josh made a clicking noise with his tongue and gently twitched the reins. His own donkey responded immediately, trotting obediently forward along the track.

"Hey! Wait for me!" Olly called. "I can't get mine started!" She leaned close to the donkey's long velvet ears. "Listen, boy," she said. "We're on a vital mission here, so could you please get going? I'll bring you an apple when we get back. Is that a deal?"

The donkey lowered its shaggy head and sniffed the ground, as if hoping to find some grass. It didn't move so much as a single hoof.

Olly watched as Josh guided his own donkey back up the path. Without speaking, he caught hold of her reins. He made a small chirruping sound, and the two donkeys began to walk along side by side.

"What are you?" Olly asked with a hushed laugh. "Josh the donkey whisperer or something?"

Josh laughed. "They trust me," he told her. "Animals are smart like that. What can I say?"

Olly smiled, then yawned. "Whose idea was it to get up so early anyway?" she groaned.

"Yours," Josh reminded her. He clicked his tongue and the two donkeys broke into a gentle trot.

A hundred thousand stars filled the sky above, their sharp glitter beginning to fade as the first hint of dawn crept out of the east. The jagged cliffs cast long, forbidding shadows, and as the donkeys trotted down the road, Olly noticed the entrances to the old tombs gaping like black mouths in the hillsides.

Sixty-three tombs had been found in the valley — sixty-three tombs for sixty-three dead pharaohs, Olly thought. She glanced over her shoulder and shivered. In the predawn gloom and silence of the canyon, it was almost possible to believe that wicked, age-old eyes were watching their progress from those dark holes in the cliffs. She was glad a few minutes later when they left the mountains behind and began the descent through the lush green fields that surrounded the town of New Gurna.

It took them about half an hour to reach the Baladi ferry dock. By then, the eastern sky was filling with light. While Josh paid the ferryman, Olly looked back again. The phantoms of the valley had been banished by the dawn, and the cliffs glowed golden in the clear light.

The water rippled under the ferry as it crossed the great river. The trip across the Nile only took a few minutes, and soon the ferry docked on the east bank and the few early passengers disembarked. Olly and

Josh paid a boy to look after their donkeys. From here they would walk.

They skirted the ruins of Luxor Temple with its massive, towering walls and impressive granite statues of Ramses II. From there, they made their way along the Sharia Cleopatra to the Midan al-Mahatta. The souk, a daily market near the center of the city, was already beginning to bustle. It was a maze of canvas-covered stalls selling a huge variety of goods: handwoven rugs, jewelry, brass- and copperware, appliqué wall hangings, leather, perfumes, exotic musical instruments. And seemingly at every step they took, there was a smiling street hawker or a vendor calling out to them to buy something.

"*La! La! Imshi!*" Josh said to a particularly persistent boy who was clawing at his clothes and begging for money. Josh had learned the phrase that meant *No! No! Go away!* from his brother the first time they visited the souk.

"Keep on the lookout for a stall that sells spices," Olly reminded him.

They made their way slowly through the narrow alleys. All around them were men in the loose-fitting galabia robes, old women wearing black with covered heads, and younger women in long gowns of brightly colored cotton.

The clamor of the bartering and talking and shouting was so loud that the two friends could hardly hear themselves think. And that wasn't their only problem. They soon came to a long, winding alley filled with the sights and scents of a hundred different spices, herbs, and dyes. They lay in heaped pyramids — warm yellow saffron, fiery red paprika, and glowing ocher curries. Baskets were stuffed with dates and figs and nuts, oranges and limes and pomegranates. Then there were juicy tomatoes, fragrant bunches of aromatic coriander and mint, piles of green peppers, onions and garlic bulbs, and huge tubs filled with rice.

Josh looked at Olly. He knew if he had really thought this through, he would have found a hundred flaws in their plan. "Which stall belongs to Khaled, do you think?"

Olly blinked at the bewildering scene in front of her. "I don't have a clue," she said helplessly. "Now what should we do?"

"Maybe we should just ask?" Josh suggested.

"No." Olly shook her head. "We need to keep out of sight. Ahmed could turn up at any minute."

"What if we split up?" Josh said. "You can hide at this end of the row, and I'll go and hide at the other. Ahmed will have to come past one of us. Then we can keep tabs on him till he does the deal."

Olly nodded. "Good plan," she agreed. She looked around. An old stallholder in dark blue robes was seated among heaps of oranges and bananas and tomatoes. Behind him, wicker baskets were stacked high. Olly walked down alongside the stall, then slipped behind the stacks of baskets and disappeared from sight. Through the lattice of wickerwork, she watched as Josh made his way quickly along the winding corridor of stalls and vanished.

Olly kept very still, breathing in the bewildering mix of exotic scents and studying the dark faces of the stallholders, wondering which one might be Khaled.

Minutes passed. More people came into the souk. Voices were raised, haggling over prices — the sellers asking too much, the buyers offering too little — in the age-old way of a bartering culture. She found the whole thing fascinating, and was quite surprised when she glanced at her watch and realized she had been waiting for fifteen minutes already.

Hunger pangs reminded her that they had set off on this trip without bringing anything to eat. Bananas were piled temptingly within arm's reach of the baskets. A banana or two would make a pleasant snack, Olly thought, but she couldn't just take them without paying.

She felt in her pockets and drew out some Egyptian money. Then she reached cautiously through the barrier of baskets and helped herself to a couple of bananas, carefully placing the money on top of the remaining pile.

She had eaten the first banana and was in the middle of peeling the second, when she saw Ahmed. Her heart jumped. He walked along the row of stalls and stopped at the one right next to her hiding place.

Olly hardly dared breathe as she watched him. He spoke to the stallholder, calling him Khaled! She grinned. She was in exactly the right place to see and hear everything. She kept as quiet and still as she could and watched Ahmed chatting with Khaled — apparently just passing the time of day.

A couple of minutes had gone by, when a tall thin man in a T-shirt and faded jeans approached the stall. He was much darker than the locals — Olly guessed he might be Ethiopian or Somali.

Ahmed greeted him with a handshake. "Are you Ghedi?" he asked, speaking in English. The man nodded. "Good," Ahmed said. "I have been waiting for you." Olly assumed that this new man either didn't speak Arabic, or spoke in a dialect that Ahmed didn't understand. English was often used as an intermediary language.

Ahmed led the man between the stalls. Olly held her breath and backed stealthily away as they approached her hiding place. She hastily squeezed herself into a narrow space between rough wooden trestles, edging deeper into cover, anxious not to ruin everything by being seen. A tap on the shoulder made her jump and whirl around. It was Josh.

Her heart pounding, Olly put her finger to her lips and gestured toward the two men. Josh nodded and they listened in silence. Ahmed and the other man were conversing in low voices, but the friends could just hear what was being said.

"You have no work permit?" Ahmed asked.

Ghedi shook his head.

"I can help you, I believe," Ahmed told him. "The English will not normally hire anyone without the correct papers, but I can tell them you are a relation of mine and give you a job in the canteen. The pay is not high, and you will need to reimburse me for my efforts on your behalf. You will give me twenty-five percent of your wages. Is that understood?"

Ghedi nodded. Ahmed smiled and took his hand. "Then we have a deal — and I have a new assistant," he said. "Come. If anyone asks, you are my distant cousin from Abu Simbel. You will work hard, but the food is free." The two men shook hands and laughed before Ahmed led Ghedi away.

Olly turned to Josh. "He was only hiring someone without a work permit," she groaned. "I got up early for nothing!"

Josh's face showed his disappointment. "I suppose we'd better get back to camp," he sighed. "If we're gone too long, we'll be in trouble."

As they crawled from their hiding space, the merchant in charge of the stall spotted them.

"Harami, harami!" the man shouted in an angry voice. He pointed to the half-peeled banana in Olly's hand. "*Harami!*" he shouted, reaching down to grab them. "*El-Ha'ni! Harami!*"

Olly recognized the words: *Thief! Help! Thief!*

"No! We're not thieves!" Olly yelled, squirming away from his grasping fingers. "I left some money — honestly, I did!" She rubbed her fingers together as a motion for money.

But the stallholder clearly didn't understand English — and he was very angry. He was shouting now, calling out names: "Essam! Bashir!" Olly had no idea how they'd explain themselves without a translator, and no one from the dig site even knew they were there.

The two friends backed away from the old man, only to find that two large, younger men had appeared behind them. Olly had no idea how they'd explain themselves without a translator, and no one from the dig site even knew they were there.

"Run!" Olly yelled. She bobbed under the grasping arms of one of the men and dived to one side. Josh was only a second behind her, slipping past the other man, just out of reach. People were stopping and staring now. Essam and Bashir were shouting as they pursued the escaping friends.

"I paid for the bananas!" Olly yelled. But the continued shouts of her pursuers made it clear her words had not been understood by their accusor.

The two friends ran, ducking and weaving between people, threading their way along the crowded alley, gasping for breath as they ran helter-skelter away from the pursuing men. They jumped over mounds of fruit and vegetables and pounded through stalls draped with colorful robes and embroidered rugs and tapestries. They were trying to find a way out of the souk, but they soon got hopelessly lost in the maze of tangled alleyways. Every street seemed blocked by crowds, and in every direction there were more stalls and more people.

They hurried along a narrow street. There were stalls on one side and sand-colored, single-story shops on the other. Josh pointed toward a small side street.

"Yes!" Olly gasped, desperate to get out of the labyrinth of the souk. They plunged headfirst down the side street. On one side there was a doorway, screened by a striped awning. Josh grabbed Olly by the arm and dived through the entrance.

The friends came to a halt and looked around. They were in a large, dark storeroom of some kind. Carpets and baskets of all shapes and sizes were stacked in profusion, alongside huge pottery urns, carved furniture, and gleaming brass ornaments. Josh dragged Olly down behind a large wooden chest. Panting as quietly as they could, the friends listened carefully for their pursuers. Soon they heard familiar loud, angry voices outside the front of the building.

It was Essam and Bashir — still close on their trail.

"We can't keep running," Josh whispered. "We have to hide." He pointed to some carpet rolls that were heaped nearby. "I know," he said, jumping up and quickly unrolling one of the carpets. "Lie on this!"

Olly stared at him in confusion. "What?"

"Just do it!" Josh panted. "Trust me. Mom did it once in a movie." He pointed to a large papyrus basket with a lid. "I'll hide in there," he said. "Now, hurry up!"

With deep misgivings, Olly lay down on the carpet. Josh grasped the edge of the rug and pulled it up over her. Olly felt Josh heave at the carpet, and then she was being rolled over and over in complete darkness.

She came to a stop face up — fortunately — but totally cocooned by the weight of the carpet. Her arms were pinned to her sides and the heavy material pressed against her face, filling her nose with the smell of newly woven wool. She couldn't move. She could barely breathe! And her nose itched!

She heard Josh's voice coming from one end of the carpet roll. "Are you OK?" he hissed.

"Barely," Olly gasped. "Hide yourself!"

She lay in the suffocating silence for a few moments, hoping that Josh would have time to get under cover. She twisted her head to get her mouth into a position where she could breathe more easily, and saw a patch of light about three feet above her — the end of the roll. Then she heard voices and the sound of footsteps. Their pursuers were just outside the room.

As Olly lay there listening to Essam and Bashir's angry voices, she realized that she was now completely helpless. She was trapped.

Chapter Four: The Plot

Once Josh was sure that Olly was safely out of sight in the rolled-up carpet, he ran for the big papyrus basket, yanked the lid off, and jumped inside. He fitted the lid back in place as well as he could, trying to breathe quietly and hoping that his heart was not beating as loudly as it sounded in his own ears.

Moments after he had secured the lid, he heard Essam and Bashir enter the room, speaking rapidly in Arabic. Soon he could hear other voices, too. Josh guessed that they belonged to the owners of the shop. The conversation rose and fell for a while. Josh didn't know much Arabic so he had no idea what was being said, but he guessed that the main subject was the two young vagabonds who had absconded from the old man's stall.

Eventually the voices moved away. It sounded as if Bashir and Essam were convinced that there were no thieves hiding inside. Josh let out a quiet sigh of relief. He was about to climb out of the basket when he heard new voices approaching. He ducked down again, groaning inwardly and hoping that these newcomers would pass by.

He was out of luck. The voices got louder: Two men, speaking in English, entered the room. Josh could hear that one had an Arabic accent, but the other sounded American.

"We can speak freely here," said the Arab. "The owner is a friend of mine — he will say nothing."

"Will he want a cut of the money?" the American demanded, his voice low and suspicious.

"A small token, that is all," replied the Arab. "A trifle. Once our friend in Cairo pays us what he has promised, there will be enough to satisfy everyone."

"Do you have the stone with you?" the American asked.

"No," responded the Arab. "But it is safe."

The American's voice grew harsh. "What do you mean? Where is it?"

"Have no fear, my friend," the Arab said quickly. "I have hidden it away — in the last place they would think to look: in the tomb of Setiankhra."

Josh held his breath, his mind reeling from what he was hearing. The two men were discussing the Elephantine Stone!

"Are you crazy?" the American snarled. "That place is crawling with people."

"I'll get it for you after nightfall, when the tomb is deserted," said the Arab. "I'll bring it to you then."

"No!" snapped the American. "That's too late. My orders are to hand it over in Cairo this evening. You fool! Why didn't you bring it with you?"

"It was too dangerous."

The American's voice came again, quiet but savage. "I gave my word that he'd have the stone today," he growled. "He doesn't accept excuses. If I let him down, bad things will happen to me." His voice became deadly. "And if bad things happen to *me*, I'll make sure bad things happen to *you*. Understand?"

"Between noon and two in the afternoon, the tomb will be empty." The Arab gasped. He sounded half-choked — as though the American had a stranglehold on him. "The diggers rest at the height of the day then. I'll get the stone for you."

"No. I'll come for it myself," the American growled. "I don't trust you to get this done right."

"But you won't be allowed into the tomb," protested the Arab. "The professor is very cautious — especially since the theft."

"Let me worry about that," replied the American. "I'll be waiting for you in the tomb at midday. Just make sure you're there with the stone. Got that?"

The Arab gasped. Josh assumed he had been released by the brutal American. "I'll be there." He lowered his voice. "Do you have the money?"

"You'll get your share, but not till he gets the stone," said the American. "Now, get lost!"

Muttering a few final words, the Arab left. Josh listened intently, waiting in cramped silence for the American to leave, too. But the man seemed in no hurry. Josh could hear subdued movements — the rustle of cellophane, the faint snap of a cigarette lighter. Then a weight came down on the basket and Josh was squashed into an even smaller space. The American was clearly sitting on Josh's hiding place!

Josh could smell cigarette smoke and hear the man muttering to himself, but he couldn't make out what the man was saying. He bit his lip, his neck aching from the unnatural position he was in. But the agony didn't last long. The American stood up and Josh heard his footsteps moving away.

Josh heaved the lid off his basket and tumbled out. He rubbed his aching legs, crouching on his hands and knees as the numbness in his feet gave way to maddening pins and needles. He tried to stand up, but his deadened feet wouldn't obey, so he crawled over to the pile of rolled carpets. "Olly?" he whispered loudly. "Are you OK?"

“Not really!” came a muffled reply. “Get me out of here!”

Josh got up onto his knees and grasped the edge of the carpet. Then, new voices made him turn in alarm. Someone was approaching and there was not enough time for him to reach the basket. He tried to scramble to his feet, but fell. In desperation, he crawled up the pile of carpets and burrowed down between two of them. He had just gotten himself out of sight when he heard cheerful voices enter the room.

Someone barked orders in Arabic, and Josh felt the heap of rolled carpets shift under him. He lifted his head and peeped out.

Two men were walking out of the room carrying a carpet between them. Josh had to stifle a groan of dismay. The men were carrying off the carpet in which Olly was still hiding!

Quickly, Josh eased himself out of his hiding place and scrambled down the pile of carpets. He ran to the doorway — his feet were working now, although they buzzed and stung as though swarming with wasps — and peered outside. At the end of the narrow side street, he could see a waiting truck. The carpet had been loaded onto the back along with some furniture and ornamental pieces. Josh stared in horror as he heard the truck’s engine splutter to life.

Ignoring the tingling in his feet, Josh ran faster than he had ever run in his life. The truck was just pulling away as he made a flying leap for the backboard. His feet dragged for a few seconds as he struggled to pull himself on board, but with a final supreme effort, he managed to haul himself up over the backboard and fall, sprawling, into the back of the truck.

It took him a few minutes to get his breath back. Then he crawled over to Olly's carpet and pulled one end open. "Are you OK?" he called.

"No!" came the muffled reply. "What's going on?"

"We're in the back of a truck."

"I figured that out for myself!" replied Olly's exasperated voice. "Unroll me!"

Josh tried to unwrap the carpet, but it was wedged between two heavy pieces of furniture. He put his mouth to the end again. "I can't. Can you wriggle out?" he asked.

"No! I can't move. I can hardly breathe!"

He reached into the roll and felt Olly's hair under his fingers. He decided that trying to drag her out by her hair wasn't a good idea — but maybe the other end?

The truck was picking up speed now, bouncing and jolting over the uneven roads as it headed south out of the town. Josh clambered down to the other end of the carpet and reached inside. He felt a shoe.

"Olly?" he called into the roll. "I'm going to pull. You try and help me." He got a firm grip on the shoe. "On the count of three," Josh shouted. "One . . . two . . . three!" He pulled with all his strength — and almost fell off the back of the truck as the shoe suddenly came off in his hand!

Defeated, he went back to the head of the carpet. "Olly? You'll have to stay where you are till the truck stops," he called. "Sorry."

"I'll make *you* sorry when I get out of here!" came the muted response.

Josh did his best to make himself comfortable. They had left the town behind now and the truck was moving rapidly along an open road. He had the horrible feeling that this might take a while!

~~~

Josh was right. It was half an hour before they came to a small village. The truck pulled off the main road and began to negotiate small side streets. Eventually, it pulled up outside a large, two-storey house, and the driver and his assistant got out and went to the front door.

Josh slipped quietly over the side of the truck and watched from behind a low wall. The front door
~~~

swung open, there was a brief conversation, and then the backboard of the van was lowered and Olly's carpet was carried, shoulder-high, into the house.

~~~~

Olly could guess what was going on. She felt herself tipping at an odd angle, and then the carpet roll jackknifed, folding her up with it. But the change helped. She was finally able to free her arms from their confined position at her sides. She dragged them up across her chest and fought to stretch them out above her head. She had just managed this exhausting feat when the carpet straightened out again, and she was sent crashing to the floor with a jolt that knocked the wind out of her.

Olly listened for a few moments and heard voices receding. She gave a sigh of relief. She was worried they might unroll the carpet right then and there. But it seemed they were happy to leave it rolled up for the time being. She waited a few moments — no voices, so she hoped, no people. She squirmed onto her stomach and began to wriggle slowly along the roll.

Now that her arms were up above her head, it was much easier for Olly to move. It only took her half a minute to get out. She wiped the fluff and sweat off her face, delighted to be free at last.
~~~~

"Phew!" she breathed, feeling slightly dizzy. "Josh goes in the carpet next time!"

She hobbled awkwardly across the room in her remaining shoe, then decided it would be easier to go barefoot and kicked it off. The other, she assumed, was still on the truck where Josh had removed it.

She was in a bedroom. Olly guessed that it belonged to a wealthy woman, because the bed was draped with colorful silks, the dressing table littered with perfumes and cosmetics. She crept to the open door, keeping herself out of sight and listening intently. It didn't sound like there was anyone nearby. It was time to make her escape from the house. She eased the door open, and almost let out a howl of shock as she came face to face with Josh!

Hurriedly, he pushed her back into the bedroom. "We can't get out that way," he whispered fiercely. "They're coming. I barely slipped past."

"You should have stayed outside," Olly told him.

"I thought you needed rescuing," Josh replied.

Olly grinned. "Thanks, but I managed to rescue myself." She sighed. "And now we *both* need rescuing."

A quick glance round the room soon told her that the window was the only other possible exit. She padded across the floor and flung it open.

"There's a trellis," she said softly. "We can climb down."

Josh tiptoed over. A thick-limbed old fig vine climbed the trellis, making it easy enough for the friends to scramble down. Josh clambered over the windowsill. Olly followed.

"What about your shoe?" Josh asked, looking up and noticing Olly's bare feet above him.

"One shoe's not much use," she replied. "You lost the other one."

"No. I have it in my pocket," Josh said.

Olly rolled her eyes. "*Now* you tell me." She edged back up the vine.

"Olly — no!" gasped Josh, but he knew it wouldn't make any difference.

Olly clambered in through the window, ran across the room and scooped up her shoe. As she was turning to leave, a group of people came in. They looked like a family — a husband, a wife, and two young daughters — and they stared at her in surprise.

Olly waved her shoe at them. "I just came back for this," she explained. "It's a really nice carpet — I hope you enjoy it more than I did," she added, as she raced back to the window.

The man stared at her, then began to speak in rapid Arabic.

Olly didn't stay to listen. She slipped lithely over the windowsill and came down the vine like a monkey.

Four astonished faces stared from the window above as the two friends sprinted along the road and disappeared around a corner.

"Well, that wasn't exactly how I expected things to go this morning," Olly gasped. "But at least we'll be able to catch that American when he turns up to get the stone." She grinned. "I think we did a pretty good job, considering!"

Josh looked at her. "We still have to get back to the dig before midday, or it'll be too late," he pointed out.

Olly nodded. She looked around. "Where exactly are we?" she asked.

Josh frowned. "The middle of nowhere," he replied and pointed. "Luxor is off in that direction. How are we going to get back in time?"

Olly gave him a determined look. "Maybe we can hitch a ride," she said. "Come on — we've got to make tracks if we're going to stop those thieves from getting away with the Elephantine Stone!"

Chapter Five: Danger from the Past

The sun shone down fiercely from high in the clear blue sky, making the road shimmer in the heat. The Nile lay to the left, silver and sparkling, and a rugged, stony emptiness stretched away to the right for as far as the eye could see. Flies buzzed, and the wheels of the cart rumbled on the road as the donkey trotted steadily along.

Olly sat perched among sacks of beans, chatting away amiably in English to the uncomprehending driver, who gazed out between the donkey's long ears at the endless road ahead.

Josh was nested farther back in the cart, lying back on the sacks and squinting in the dazzling light. "You do realize he can't understand a single word you're saying, don't you?" Josh pointed out.

"I'm sure he recognizes that I'm being friendly," Olly replied. "That's what counts." She looked back. "What time is it?"

Josh glanced at his watch. "It's almost ten thirty."

Olly frowned. They had been on the cart for half

the morning, and there was still no sign of Luxor. The driver, a small, wizened man with only two teeth in his wide smile, had been happy to give them a lift. But Olly had been unable to explain in her broken Arabic that they were in a desperate hurry and had to get back to the Valley of the Kings by midday at the latest.

She decided to try again. "Excuse me."

The driver looked around at her and let out a laughing stream of Arabic. He seemed to find Olly very amusing.

"I'm glad I'm so entertaining," she said patiently. "But is there any way your lovely donkey could be persuaded to go just a little bit faster?"

The driver chuckled and nodded, but nothing happened.

"That's it," Olly said, throwing her arms in the air. "I give up."

"The donkey's probably doing its best," Josh said. "How would *you* like to be hauling us around in this heat?"

"You're right," Olly agreed. "But it drives me crazy when cars and trucks go flying past, leaving us in a cloud of dust. I feel like I've been on this road *forever.*" She turned and gazed ruefully at the winding road.

Josh squirmed around on the sacks, trying to get

more comfortable. The donkey trotted on. Time trickled by.

It was a few minutes before noon when they finally got back to the ferry dock. The boy was still there with their donkeys. They had told him they would only be an hour and he was angry at having been stuck there all morning, so they apologized profusely and gave him all the money they still had in their pockets, save their ferry fare. He counted it carefully, then broke into a wide smile and ran off, leaving them with the donkeys.

The ferry was crowded with tourists now. It was approaching the hottest part of the day, and most of the locals were resting in the shade.

Before long, Olly and Josh were across the river and riding back to camp on their donkeys. They were both relieved when they rode up through New Gurna and finally saw the mountain ridges of the Valley of the Kings looming ahead of them.

~~~

They dropped the donkeys off with Abdullah and ran toward the trailers. Olly noticed a few diggers sitting in the shade, resting. A trailer door opened as they approached, and Olly's gran stepped down, her head shaded by a wide-brimmed straw hat. Olly could sense trouble ahead.
~~~

"I want a word with you two!" her gran said sternly. "We were worried sick until Abdullah told us you'd borrowed two donkeys for a trip to Luxor. What on earth have you been up to?"

"I'm sorry, Gran," Olly gasped. "There's no time to explain. Where's Dad? It's really, really important."

"Your father has driven down to the other end of the valley to do some research in another tomb," her gran replied.

"What about Jonathan?" Josh asked.

"He's working in the office trailer," Mrs. Beckmann said. "But I wouldn't disturb him if I were you — you're not exactly the flavor of the month right now."

"Can't help that, Gran," Olly put in. "We've got vital information." She and Josh ran over to the trailer that had been set up as the site office. Audrey Beckmann followed.

Olly was first through the trailer door, closely followed by Josh. They burst in to find Jonathan frowning over calculations on his laptop. The screen showed a 3-D plan of Setiankhra's tomb as excavated so far.

Jonathan glared at them. "You guys are in so much trouble," he growled as Audrey Beckmann appeared in the doorway behind them.

"But we know where the stone is!" Josh blurted out.

"So *that's* it!" Mrs. Beckmann said. "I should have known."

Jonathan stared at the friends. "What are you talking about?" he demanded, his face grim. "I told you two to stop all this nonsense."

"Yes, but we found out that the stone has been here all along!" Olly explained. "It was stashed in Setiankhra's tomb. And an American man is coming here today — right now — to get it and take it to a buyer in Cairo! If we don't do something quickly, the stone will be gone for good!"

Jonathan stared at her. "An American?" he repeated. "Did you say an American?"

"Yes!" Olly and Josh exclaimed together.

"An American newspaper reporter was here just a few minutes ago," Jonathan said. He looked at Audrey Beckmann. "He told me he wanted to write a big piece on the tomb. He asked if he could take a look around." His eyes widened in shocked realization. "He's in there right now!"

"I'll call the police," Olly's gran said, moving to the desk and picking up the telephone.

Olly shook her head. "They won't get here in time," she pointed out. "We have to stop him *now!*"

"She's right," Jonathan said, jumping up and running for the door. "I'll make sure he doesn't get away!"

Olly glanced at her gran and saw that she was completely immersed in her telephone call. Grabbing Josh by the arm, Olly dived for the door.

"Come on," she said in a fierce whisper. "Jonathan might need help!"

Josh didn't need any encouragement. Together, they jumped down from the trailer and raced toward the tomb entrance.

Jonathan had already disappeared inside by the time Olly and Josh arrived.

Josh caught hold of Olly and brought her to a skidding halt at the entrance. "We won't help by rushing in," he said. "Keep quiet and we'll find out what's going on first."

Olly nodded and they crept silently through the entrance. A few yards down the first passageway, the electric lights began. Olly peered down the rest of the corridor, but it sloped at such a steep angle that she couldn't tell where the hallway leveled out before dropping off again.

Angry voices drifted up to her from the depths of the tomb. Olly swallowed nervously and looked at Josh. His face showed the same uneasiness.

"That is a priceless artifact," they heard Jonathan say. "I can't let you take it."

The American's reply was savage. "That's what you think. Get out of my way!" There was the sound of a scuffle.

Olly and Josh ran down the sloping corridor. An alarming sight met their eyes. Jonathan and the American were locked in a wild struggle, staggering back and forth across the floor of the chamber.

The American was a big man, taller and heavier than Jonathan, and several years older. He was wearing jeans and a brown leather jacket. He had close-cut black hair and wild, dark eyes. Behind him, Olly could see a third figure, small and slight, who she recognized instantly. His name was Habbib, and he was one of the oldest of the hired diggers. His face was tanned and wrinkled by the sun, his hair thin and gray. He clutched a bundle of cloth in his hands, and Olly guessed immediately that it was wrapped around the Elephantine Stone.

Jonathan caught sight of Olly and his brother. "Get out of here!" he gasped.

The American was quick to take advantage of his opponent's distraction. He delivered a crushing blow to the back of Jonathan's neck, which sent the younger man crashing to the floor. A vicious kick then threw Jonathan onto his side and sent him sliding a few feet or so farther down the slope, where he lay gasping and winded. The American took a step toward him.

"You leave him alone!" Olly shouted, too concerned for Jonathan's safety to care about drawing the thug's attention. The American turned toward her, his eyes glinting with menace.

"You're not getting past us!" Josh shouted, his voice shaky but determined.

A cruel grin spread over the American's face. He obviously didn't think Olly and Josh posed much of an obstacle.

Olly acted almost without thinking. The American was standing on the level area between the two sloping corridors. Close to his feet was one of the wedges that had been pushed between the booby-trap stones. Olly sprang forward and aimed a wild kick at the wedge. Her foot struck it hard, sending it skidding across the stones. With a yell of triumph, Olly threw herself backward to safety.

Panting, she stared at the American, expecting the stones to tip at any moment and send him tumbling into darkness. But nothing happened. Olly's desperate gamble had failed. The ancient system of booby traps was no longer working.

"The stone!" the American snarled, shooting a quick look over his shoulder at the terrified digger. "Give it to me!" He reached out, his feet planted firmly, his eyes on Olly and Josh.

The digger stared at him but did not move. Olly could tell from the fear in his eyes that he had not been expecting violence.

"Give me the stone!" the American shouted. Trembling, the digger crept forward and pushed the bundle into the American's hands. He glanced with troubled eyes at Olly and Josh, then backed away again.

The American clutched the bundle of cloth to his chest. His face stretched into a devious grin as he turned toward the two friends. Olly and Josh stood side by side — blocking the corridor. Olly was scared but determined. She wasn't going to let the man get past without a fight — even if the odds were hopeless.

But with his first step toward the exit, the American's foot came down awkwardly. A stone shifted under him, causing him to lose his balance and fall to the floor. At the same moment, Olly heard an eerie, rushing, hissing sound coming from the walls, accompanied by an ominous grinding noise. Her eyes widened as she wondered what was to come. Seconds later, a dozen stone spears shot from the pockmarked wall and flew across the corridor. They struck the far side, cracking and splintering into fragments. Surprised and startled, Olly threw herself to the floor, her arms coming up to shield her face from the flying shrapnel.

The American stared up in shock — if he had not fallen, the spikes would have impaled him! He staggered to his feet, his face distorted with anger as he stared down at Olly. But before he could make a move toward her, the air filled with a wild blast of fine sand. He threw his hands up to protect his face, and staggered backward, blinded and disoriented.

Olly heard the Egyptian let out a frantic stream of Arabic. She peered between her fingers and saw him cowering back from the ancient booby trap. She could see where the sand was coming from — it gushed out of the holes in the walls, cascading into the corridor like water from a burst pipe. But that was not all — blocks of stone began to rain down from the roof, thudding and crashing to the floor with deadly force.

The booby traps had come alive — and they were as lethal as on the day the pharaoh had died!

Chapter Six: The Tattoo

Olly stared at the mayhem she had created. It had never occurred to her that removing the wooden wedge would cause such chaos. As the booby traps activated around her she scrambled to her feet, deafened by the noise. She and Josh were already ankle-deep in the fine, spreading sand. Some of the falling stones were hitting the floor and crashing straight through to the depths below, their weight dislodging the stones that held the floor together. Sand poured through the gaps. More stones fell away.

Through the storm of fine sand, Olly saw Jonathan stagger to his feet and stumble toward the American, who was poised on the edge of the widening pit.

The floor seemed to be caving in. With a rumble of moving stone, a wide trench appeared in front of Olly. She jumped backward just in time, pulling Josh with her as the ground under his feet gave way.

The stones and sand were tumbling into a deep dark pit. The American was still on his feet, but he was at the heart of the area protected by the booby traps, and the flood of sand blinded him, making it impossible for him to navigate an escape. As Olly watched, the ground disappeared beneath him. As he fell in a sucking avalanche of sand, the wrapped bundle fell from his hands and thudded to the unsteady ground of the tomb.

Jonathan sprang forward and grabbed hold of the American's hand. The weight of the falling man pulled him to the very brink of the gaping pit, but by lying flat on what remained of the floor, Jonathan was able to keep hold of the American and save him from plunging into the chasm.

Olly could see the bottom of the pit far below, faintly lit by the electric light. Row upon row of sharpened stone spikes pointed upward: a deadly trap that had been waiting over three thousand years to claim its first victim.

Jonathan grabbed hold of the American's other hand and slowly hauled him up until he was able to catch hold of the edge of the pit. Relieved of the man's full weight, Jonathan was able to get to his knees, reach down, and drag him back up to ground level.

Olly could see that there was no fight left in the man. He crawled to the side of the corridor and sat with his back to the wall, breathing heavily and nursing the gash in his shoulder.

A strange quiet descended in the tomb. The torrent of sand had lessened until it was no more than a trickle from the holes in the wall. The roof was pocked with gaps left by the fallen stones, and the entire level area between the sloping corridors of the tomb was gone. Instead a gaping hole yawned, threatening to swallow up any unwary intruders.

The terrified digger was crouched against the wall, some way down the lower corridor, staring up toward the booby traps with frightened eyes and muttering anxiously under his breath.

Jonathan stood up and stared across the pit to where Olly was standing in stunned silence. "Olly," he said, wiping an arm across his sweating forehead. "You are something else!"

"I didn't realize all this would happen!" she gasped, her voice apologetic. "I just thought a stone would give way underneath him. Are you OK?"

"I'm fine." He looked around the remains of the corridor. "This place will never be the same again, though." He shook his head. "I can't figure out whether you were incredibly brave or just plain crazy!"

Olly bit her lip. He had a point! But before she could think of a response, they all heard the sound of people approaching from the entrance.

Audrey Beckmann and Mohammed appeared at the head of a group of diggers. "The police are on their way," Mrs. Beckmann said, staring at the debris. "What on earth happened down here?"

Olly blinked at her. "I set the booby traps off, Gran," she said quietly. "And they were a little more spectacular than I'd expected."

Josh looked at his friend. "What am I always telling you about not touching things?" he said. Josh's face was serious, but Olly thought she saw the hint of a grin.

Jonathan picked up the bundle of cloth from the floor and unwrapped it to reveal the Elephantine Stone, still intact. He let out a sigh of relief, holding it up for them all to see. "I think we'll let Olly get away with it this time," he said with a laugh. "What do you think?"

^^^^^

Half an hour had passed. Habbib and the subdued American were sitting on the ground with their backs to the office trailer, watched over by Mohammed the foreman and a couple of burly diggers. Habbib had his knees to his chest and his head in his hands. He was muttering constantly to himself, obviously traumatized by the events that had taken place in the tomb of Setiankhra. Documents in the American's wallet showed him to be going under the name of Benjamin Carter. He was sullen and withdrawn, offering no further information about himself and refusing offers of food and water.

Professor Christie had been contacted and was on his way back to the site from his research in the tomb of Ramses II. The police were expected at any moment.

Jonathan had led a party of diggers into the tomb to start clearing up the mess. Some kind of bridge would have to be constructed to span the chasm that the booby traps had created.

Olly and Josh were sitting with Audrey Beckmann in her trailer. Olly had the Elephantine Stone in her lap. She stroked it lightly with her fingertips. "I knew we'd find it," she said happily.

"You weren't supposed to be looking for it!" her gran said, glancing sternly from Olly to Josh. "Do you have any idea of the damage you could have done to yourselves?"

Olly looked at her. "Dad won't be mad, will he?" she asked. "After all, we did get the stone back for him."

Her gran's eyes glinted. "It's not your father you need to worry about," she said. "It's me!"

Olly gave her a weak smile. "Oh."

Audrey Beckmann looked gravely at the two friends. "You behaved recklessly and thoughtlessly," she said seriously. She frowned at Josh. "I know Olivia can't always help herself, but you're normally a little more sensible, Josh. And your brother expressly told you to stop interfering."

Olly saw Josh squirm a little under her gran's keen gaze. "We did get the stone back," he said. "You'd think people would be grateful," he added sulkily, under his breath.

"You were lucky," Audrey continued. "You could have been hurt — or even killed. You are never to do anything so foolish again — do you understand me?"

"Yes, Gran," Olly said quietly. Josh nodded.

The awkward interview was cut short by the sound of an approaching Land Rover.

"That's Dad!" Olly exclaimed.

They all came out of the trailer to meet the professor. His face was clouded as he climbed out of the Land Rover. He was clearly worried about Olly and Josh, but Olly quickly managed to convince him that they were both unhurt.

The recovery of the stone delighted the professor and he listened in amazement to Olly's description of the morning's events, and the chaos that had been caused by her activation of the tomb's booby traps.

"The whole roof fell in!" Olly exclaimed, shaking her head. "And just because I moved one little wedge. Those ancient Egyptians *really* had something against burglars!"

"I hope there wasn't too much harm done," her father said.

"Well, the American and Habbib were a little shaken up," Olly replied. "But the rest of us are fine."

Her father blinked at her. "I meant to the tomb," he said.

Olly grinned. Typical Dad!

Only a few minutes after Professor Christie's return, the police arrived to take Habbib and Benjamin Carter into custody.

"Let's hope this is an end to the matter," Professor Christie said to the officers.

Olly noticed her dad staring at the American's wrist as he was put into the back of the police vehicle. Her father was silent and thoughtful as the police car drove away. "What's wrong, Dad?" Olly asked.

He looked distractedly at her. "Very curious. That man had a tattoo on his wrist," he said. "It was the hieroglyphic symbol for Nuit." He took out a small notepad and sketched a strange serpentine symbol.

Josh leaned over Olly's shoulder to see. "What's Nuit?" he asked.

"Nuit was the mother of Isis," Olly said. "I've read about her. She was the sky goddess who swallowed the stars every morning. She also had something to do with the whole resurrection business — they used to paint a picture of her inside the lid of a sarcophagus."

"That's right," said her father, sounding even more professorial than usual. "She married the Earth god Geb, son of Ra, and she gave birth to two sons, Set and Osiris, and two daughters, Nephthys and Isis. She is a sky goddess, and a powerful protector from demons and darkness."

"Why would an American have a tattoo like that?" Josh asked.

"I have no idea," replied the professor vaguely. He gazed toward Setiankhra's tomb. "I must go and see what damage you two managed in removing the stone," he said. "I hope all this trouble isn't going to slow down our work." He slipped the notepad back into his pocket and headed for the tomb.

"I bet I can come up with plenty of explanations for that tattoo," Olly said to Josh. "For a start, that American might be a member of a secret cult, and —"

"I think we can save the guessing games till later," Audrey interrupted, having come up suddenly behind the two friends. "You're overdue for some lessons by now."

Olly stared at her. "We found the Elephantine Stone, got two criminals locked up, and we *still* have to do school work?" she said. "Unbelievable!"

^^^^^

The friends spent much of the rest of the afternoon doing their school work. They surfaced several hours later to find that, under Jonathan's supervision, a team of diggers had already constructed a temporary, plank-built bridge over the chasm in the tomb. More lights had also been installed — the corridors and the Burial Chamber were now fully illuminated.

Josh and Olly walked carefully over the wooden bridge, peering down into the shadowy depths below where the wicked stone spikes waited.

"We almost ended up down there," Josh remarked. "Ouch!"

Olly nodded but said nothing, preferring not

to think about it. Instead, she focused on the remarkable tomb decorations that the extra lights now revealed.

Despite the damage caused by centuries of flooding, the tomb was full of marvelous paintings, their colors bursting into life under the electric lights. The old dyes had held their color to an extraordinary degree. There were rich reds, emerald greens, splashes of pure white, and pools of deep black. Hieroglyphics covered the spaces between the pictures. As Professor Christie had said only a few days ago, the secrets of Setiankhra's tomb looked like they would take months of dedicated work to unravel.

Josh seemed preoccupied as he and Olly wandered back out into the late afternoon sunlight.

"Are you wondering about Carter's tattoo?" Olly asked him. "I am. I'm sure I've seen it somewhere before — only I can't remember where."

Josh shook his head. "No, it's something else," he said thoughtfully. "I didn't want to mention it in front of everyone until I thought it through, but I don't think Habbib was the same person we heard talking to the American in that storeroom in Luxor."

Olly frowned and tried to think back to what she had heard from her hiding place in the carpet. "Now that you mention it, I think you might be right," she said. "The Arab in Luxor sounded like a much younger man, didn't he?"

Josh nodded. "And someone with good English. He said he would meet up with Carter at the dig to hand over the stone, but what if he decided it was too risky to do it himself? What if he sent Habbib along instead?"

Olly's eyes widened. "If that's right, you know what it means, don't you?"

Josh looked grim. "It means the original thief could still be here — waiting for another chance," he said.

"We have to tell my dad about this," Olly declared. "Come on!"

Confronted by Olly and Josh in his trailer a few minutes later, Professor Christie listened in concerned silence. "I don't like the sound of that," he said at last. "I'll call the police and see what they have to say about it. In the meantime, Josh, would you go and find Jonathan for me? I was planning on asking him to drive up to Cairo in the morning and put the stone in a safety deposit box at the museum.

But in light of what you've just told me, I'm going to suggest he drive up there tonight."

Josh discovered Jonathan in his trailer, poring over old documents with the Elephantine Stone safely at his elbow. He agreed with the professor that the safest course of action was to get the stone as far from the camp as possible and, within the hour, he was waving good-bye as he set off in the Land Rover.

By the evening, the adventures of the day were beginning to wear on Josh and Olly. Not long after dinner, they grew tired of watching DVDs and decided to head for bed.

"Sleep well," Olly's gran said. "And remember what I told you: No more stupid risks — do you hear me?"

"Yes, Gran," Olly yawned. "I mean, no, Gran. I mean . . . oh, whatever you say, Gran."

Olly said good night to Josh, who shared the trailer next door with his brother. Then she quickly got ready for bed, switched off the light, and settled down between the sheets. She expected to be asleep in seconds, but her brain wouldn't shut down. It was as if a bright light was shining inside her head and she couldn't turn it off.

She groaned, tossing and turning uncomfortably. In her head she could see the symbol of Nuit that her father had drawn earlier that afternoon. And Nuit was the mother of Isis. She thought that might be important. After all, the talisman they were searching for was known as the Tears of Isis.

It was interesting to Olly that her father had not mentioned the talismans since arriving in the Valley of the Kings. She wondered if it was almost like a superstition, that they didn't discuss the artifacts until they had found some evidence to link them to the site.

Olly wondered what the Tears of Isis might be. She knew the word *talisman* meant some kind of charm that guaranteed good fortune or had magical powers. But the words Tears of Isis sounded enchanted all by themselves. It would be wonderful for her dad if he found this first talisman. They would be a great step closer to locating the archives and reconciling the long-standing Christie curse.

Olly's mind wandered back to the symbol of Nuit. She was sure she had seen a tattoo just like that before — but when, and where?

Olly closed her eyes and desperately tried to remember. She had an image in her mind — simple, but very precise. She could see the ground at eye level and a pair of feet under a long galabia robe. But whose feet? And why was the ground at her eye level? Because she was in a hole, she realized suddenly. And with that, the memory came into focus.

It had been days ago. She had been helping the diggers. She had been in a pit, shoveling earth into a basket, when someone had walked close to the edge, accidentally kicking sand down over her. Olly remembered standing up, ready to give them a piece of her mind — and then she had seen that it was Mohammed, the foreman. He had looked down and apologized profusely before moving away. And it was at that moment that Olly had briefly glimpsed the dark tattoo on the young man's bare ankle.

It was the serpentine symbol of Nuit. The same symbol that her dad had sketched earlier.

And the very same tattoo that Benjamin Carter had on his wrist.

Chapter Seven: Secrets Concealed and Secrets Revealed

Josh lay in pitch-darkness, listening to the deep silence of the valley. He was stretched on his back, hands behind his head, thinking over the day's extraordinary events. Jonathan's bed was empty. It was a six-hour drive to Cairo, so the plan was for Jonathan to spend the night in a hotel and hand the stone over to the museum authorities first thing in the morning. He was expected back on site some time in the afternoon.

Josh was glad that the Elephantine Stone was gone. Far better for it to be safe on the road to Cairo than locked up in the small security box that Jonathan kept by his bed. Everyone on the site knew of the box — or could easily hear about it — and Josh was certain that at least one thief was still at large.

He turned onto his side and began to drift off to sleep. But then he was shocked into wakefulness by a small, sharp sound. Josh opened his eyes in the darkness, his senses acutely alert. He was facing away from the door of the trailer, but he felt a breath of air on his cheek, as if the door was open.

Listening intently, his heart pounding, Josh heard the sound of stealthy footfalls moving slowly across the floor. Then he had the creepy sensation that someone was leaning over him. He thought it might be Jonathan, back early, but then dismissed that idea, realizing it wasn't possible — the round trip to Cairo took at least twelve hours.

The next instant Josh guessed what was happening. The thief didn't know that the stone was gone — and he had come to Jonathan's trailer looking for it! Josh realized that this was his chance to discover the thief's identity. Summoning all his courage, he surged up from the bed, grasping the blanket and throwing it over the dark figure. There was a startled squawk as Josh's full weight came down on the intruder, bearing them to the ground. They tumbled together onto the floor, Josh on top, and the thief enveloped in the folds of the blanket.

The thief struggled inside the blanket, and that was when Josh realized that something was wrong. The thief was too small!

Josh sat up, panting. He found the top of the blanket and pulled it off the face of his captive. "Olly!" he exclaimed in surprise.

"Are you crazy?" Olly gasped. "What are you doing?"

Josh rolled off her and switched on his bedside lamp. Olly stared up at him from the floor.

"I thought you were the thief," Josh explained. He saw that she was fully clothed. "What are you up to?" he asked.

Olly got up and sat on the bed. "I remembered where I've seen the Nuit tattoo before," she told Josh. "Mohammed has one exactly like it on his ankle." And she explained how she had come to see the tattoo.

Josh looked thoughtfully at her. He shook his head. "It's a coincidence. That symbol could stand for just about anything," he said. "Mohammed's a really nice person — I can't see him stealing the stone. Besides, your dad trusts him completely, doesn't he?"

Olly nodded. "He does," she agreed. "But right now that tattoo is the only lead we have. I think we should check it out."

"We?" Josh asked dubiously, remembering Mrs. Beckmann's stern words. "Are you sure?"

"Dead sure!" Olly said. "Come on, Josh, we're a great team. Look how well we did today. Are you with me or not?"

Josh sighed. Olly always knew how to get the best of his curiosity. "Count me in," he said, with a reluctant smile. "But what's our plan of action?"

"We need to find out whether Mohammed and Carter were working together, right?" Olly began. "I thought we could wait till everyone's busy at the dig tomorrow, then take a look inside Mohammed's tent."

"What do you think we'll find?"

"I'm not sure," Olly replied. "I doubt there'll be anything obvious — you know, like a diary with an incriminating entry: *Busy day today. Weather hot. Lots of digging. Stole Elephantine Stone.* Nothing like that. But I know Mohammed has a laptop computer and there might be something on that. He must have communicated with Benjamin Carter somehow — and e-mail would be the easiest way."

"You're right," Josh agreed, impressed. "That makes sense."

Olly grinned. "OK, I'm going back to bed," she said. "See you in the morning."

A few moments later, Josh watched from the window as Olly slipped back to her trailer through the quiet stillness of the desert night. It looked like tomorrow was going to be another eventful day, he thought. And if Olly's suspicions were correct, they might even find the evidence they needed to unmask the thief once and for all.

~~~~~

It was late the next morning when Olly and Josh sat down for breakfast with Olly's gran. They ate at a table set up by her trailer, shaded by a wide umbrella. Mrs. Beckmann was reading *The Times* — two days old — brought in from England.

Olly poured honey over the yogurt and granola in her bowl and stirred it thoughtfully with a spoon. Josh yawned a lot — still not fully recovered from the activity of the previous day.

Audrey Beckmann lowered her newspaper and peered at the two friends. "So," she said. "Did you both sleep well?"

"Out like a light," Olly said, not meeting her gaze. "Straight to bed and straight to sleep, as per instructions."

"Me, too," Josh said. "Has Jonathan called yet?"

"He spoke on the phone to Olly's father a couple of hours ago when he was about to take the stone into the museum. He said to expect him back some time midafternoon," Olly's gran responded.

"Where's Dad?" Olly asked.

"Your father's been in Setiankhra's tomb for an hour or more already," Mrs. Beckmann said,
~~~~~

nodding toward the distant entrance. "And he was up studying old papers till really late last night."

"Is Mohammed with him?" Olly asked innocently.

"I think so," Mrs. Beckmann replied. "Your father took quite a big team over there with him."

Olly looked significantly at Josh. The coast was clear for them to put their plan into operation. She finished her breakfast and pushed the bowl away.

"I think I'll go for a stroll," she said, stretching her arms above her head. "Coming, Josh?"

"OK," he said, bolting the last of his breakfast. "I'll be right behind you."

Mrs. Beckmann looked at them. "What are you two planning?" she asked.

"Nothing," Olly said. "You've got such a suspicious mind, Gran. Why would we be planning anything?"

The older woman's eyebrows lifted. "I meant, what do you intend to do with yourselves this morning?" she said.

"Oh." Olly blinked at her. "Nothing special. This and that."

"Just remember what I told you," her gran warned.

Olly and Josh looked at each other, and Josh nodded to indicate they should make their escape before Mrs. Beckmann started asking more questions.

They had just left the table when one of the diggers, a cheerful young man named Fasal, came running from the tomb entrance. The professor wanted them. "The professor — very excited," Fasal explained as the three of them followed him back to the tomb. "He find writings — on wall. Very good writings — very important, he says."

"I wonder what it is," Olly murmured, but she was thinking that it must have something to do with the Tears of Isis. Only that, or the sarcophagus of Setiankhra would get him that excited.

Professor Christie and Mohammed were in the Burial Chamber. The professor was crouched on the floor with a notepad on his knee, copying hieroglyphics from the wall, lit by a flashlight that Mohammed was holding.

Olly looked at the handsome young Egyptian. He met her eyes and smiled, and Olly felt slightly ashamed for suspecting him of stealing. Maybe her theory was a bit far-fetched.

Professor Christie stood up, his face eager and flushed. "It was sheer luck," he told them excitedly. "I had only been working for a short time when I discovered this." He pointed to the hieroglyphics.

Olly and Josh peered at them. As far as they could tell, the glyphs were no different from all the other writings that covered the walls of the chamber.

The professor pointed to part of the writing. "This is the name of Nuit — not the single symbol we were talking about yesterday, that's just a kind of shorthand — this is the full name. It reads: *Nuit, mother of Isis, lays her blessings upon you, wise wanderer in the winding pathways of the world.*" His voice trembled with excitement. "*I open the chambers of my heart to you.*" He turned to the three, his eyes shining. "And then it says: *You who would gather the tears of my daughter must first unlock the many doors of my house.* Do you see? It must refer to the Tears of Isis. There's no other interpretation. The words in these hieroglyphs are intended to lead straight to that particular Talisman of the Moon!"

"Have you translated the rest?" Olly's gran asked.

"I have," said the professor. He glanced down at his notepad. "It seems to be in the form of a riddle."

Mohammed spoke. "My ancestors often hid their great secrets in riddles and puzzles," he said. "That way, only the wise and the worthy could understand them."

"What does it say?" Josh asked.

The professor read aloud from his notes. As he spoke, his voice seemed to grow stronger and deeper, booming through the empty chambers and echoing in the long corridors of stone. "*In the Chamber of Light, the room that devours itself, the sacred two of the air, and the sacred four of the almond eyes, and the sacred six in black armor shall unite beneath the sacred seven. And the light of the sacred seven will shine upon the head that is whole and the heart that is awake and the eyes that weep.*"

A strange, breathless silence followed.

"Wow!" Olly said softly. "That's amazing."

"Could we have a copy of that?" Josh asked. "I'd like to try and figure it out, if that's okay. Just for fun."

"Certainly," the professor said. "But even if you can solve the riddle, we're still left with another puzzle."

"Let me guess," Olly said. "How do we find 'the room that devours itself'?"

Her father nodded. "Yes. For starters." He turned to Mohammed. "We have more work to do," he said. "Let's hope our luck holds. At least we know one thing for certain: The clues on the Elephantine Stone were genuine — the Tears of Isis talisman is apparently somewhere in this tomb!"

~~~

Olly and Josh walked toward the encampment where the tents belonging to Mohammed, and
~~~

several of the other diggers, had been pitched. Those diggers who had been recruited locally — from Luxor, New Gurna, and the nearby towns of Armant, Razagat, and Qus — went home at nightfall. But at least a dozen diggers had come from as far away as Aswan or Cairo. They had formed a little camp near to the canteen run by Ahmed. It was hidden from the main excavation site by a thrusting shoulder of the hills.

"What do you think a 'room that devours itself' can be?" Olly asked. "It's just plain *weird*, if you ask me."

"I don't know yet," replied Josh. He frowned. "But I've heard something like it before." Josh might have said he wanted a copy of the riddle just for fun, but he was determined to figure it out. He liked this kind of challenge. Besides, he was good at it.

"I've been thinking," Olly said. "What if the tattoos are a complete coincidence?"

"Then we won't find anything," Josh said simply. He looked at Olly curiously. "Have you changed your mind about searching Mohammed's tent?"

"Well, no," Olly wavered. "I guess not. I just feel a little awkward about it, that's all." She chewed her lip thoughtfully. "The tattoo *is* suspicious, though," she said firmly. "We should check it out. Let's get it over with." She looked around. They were on the outskirts of the small camp. "Which tent belongs to Mohammed?"

Josh pointed at the largest tent. "That one," he said.

"One of us should keep watch," Olly suggested, looking back the way they had come. "Are you OK with that, while I go and investigate?"

Josh nodded. "I'll give you a call if I see anyone heading this way," he said. He clambered up the hump of rock and peered over the top. From this vantage point he could see anyone coming in plenty of time. He turned and gave Olly the thumbs up.

Olly unzipped the flap of Mohammed's tent and crawled inside, pulling the zipper down again behind her. The air was stuffy under the sloping canvas. A simple bed took up one side, and a few personal items sat on a small folding table: one or two books, shaving gear, an oil lamp. On the groundsheet, clothes and other basic items were laid out in neat piles.

Olly looked around quickly for the laptop. She found it on the bed, half-covered by a fold of the blanket. She pulled it out and knelt on the floor to open it and switch it on. The screen lit up.

Olly felt uncomfortable — her conscience was still pricking her. What if Mohammed was totally innocent? What if she'd gotten it all wrong? "He'll never know," she whispered to herself firmly. "Now I'm here, I might just as well get on with it."

There were several folders and icons on the computer screen, most of which seemed to concern Mohammed's university studies, and similar archaeological and historical subjects. Olly rolled the mouse-ball and clicked on the envelope icon to run the e-mail program.

There were lots of e-mails in the inbox and they had all been read. They came from various places — from individuals, from Cairo University, and from several international museums as well. Olly was about to start reading them when a new e-mail arrived.

The sender was *ec@moon-phase.net.* She opened the mail. It was brief, with no greeting and no sign-off at the end. *How does our enterprise fare? Your ten-percent share in the venture is in jeopardy unless things are resolved quickly. I have other contacts willing to take over if you cannot fulfill your part of the deal. Respond immediately.*

Olly raised an eyebrow. Someone out there wasn't very happy with Mohammed right now. He was obviously involved in a business deal that wasn't going smoothly. But did it have anything to do with the Elephantine Stone? The e-mail was too vague for Olly to tell one way or the other.

Olly decided to read a few more e-mails. Now that she looked, there were several from the same address: *ec@moon-phase.net*. They might shed some light on the mystery.

But she didn't get a chance to read any other e-mails because she was interrupted by a frantic voice from outside the tent. It was Josh. "It's Mohammed!" she heard him call. "He's coming! Olly, get out of there, now!"

Chapter Eight: The Riddle of Nuit

Josh had been daydreaming — gazing up at the cliffs surrounding the Valley of the Kings and turning the phrase "the room that devours itself" over in his mind. He hadn't thought for one moment that anyone would actually come over to the camp at this time of day. He had expected them all to be busy in the tomb. It was lucky that he happened to peer over the hump of rock and see Mohammed walking in his direction. The young Egyptian was already alarmingly close.

Panicking, Josh slid down the bulge of rock and raced for Mohammed's tent. He called a warning to Olly, then turned and sprinted back the way he had come. If he was quick, he would be able to head Mohammed off before he rounded the shoulder of rock. That would give Olly more time to make her getaway — and make up for not keeping a more careful watch.

In fact, Josh almost crashed into Mohammed and made him jump.

“Hello,” Josh said breathlessly.

“Hello, Josh,” Mohammed replied with a smile. “You are in a hurry, I see.”

“Not really,” Josh began, thinking fast. “Actually, I’m glad I bumped into you. I’ve been thinking about that riddle in the tomb. Do you have any idea what it might mean?”

“I’ve not had time to think about it,” Mohammed responded. “But such things were the delight of my ancient ancestors. Far wiser men than I have spent entire lifetimes trying to solve the old riddles.” He smiled. “This is an ancient country, Josh. Its sands hide many ancient secrets. Some may never be solved.” He nodded politely. “Forgive me, I have to get something from my tent.” He sidestepped Josh and continued on.

Josh turned to walk alongside him. “I could get it for you,” he offered.

“That’s kind of you, but unnecessary,” Mohammed said. “It will only take me a moment.”

They were just outside the tent now. Mohammed stooped, drew up the zipper and slipped inside. Josh closed his eyes, fearing disaster. But nothing happened. He opened his eyes again and saw something at the edge of his vision: a small, rapidly moving shape.

It was Olly, running at full speed for the cover of the rocks. She had gotten out in time.

^^^^^

"Phew!" Olly gasped. "That was close." She looked at Josh, her eyes narrowing. "How did that happen?" she demanded. "You should have been able to see him from way off. I bet you weren't keeping close enough watch!"

"Of course I was," Josh answered defensively. "Anyway, did you find the laptop?"

"I did," Olly said. "Although I only had time for a quick look."

"Was there anything useful?" Josh asked.

Olly frowned. "Not really. There was one e-mail that seemed a bit odd." She explained about the mail from moon-phase.net. "And there were others from the same person, but I didn't get a chance to look at them. When you yelled, I just had time to mark the mail as unread and put the laptop back where I found it."

"So, we're no closer to finding out whether Mohammed and Carter were working together," Josh mused. "Maybe we should take another look in Mohammed's tent?"

Olly shook her head. "I don't think that's such a

great idea," she said. "We barely got away with it the first time. I'm still shaking!"

"So, what do we do now?" Josh asked.

"Let's get a copy of that riddle," Olly suggested. "If we put our heads together, we might be able to crack it." She grinned at Josh. "Wouldn't it be something if we worked out how to find the Tears of Isis before Dad and Jonathan did?"

~~~~

Olly and Josh sat at the table by the trailer, eating lunch. Each had a notepad and a pen. The translation of the riddle lay in the middle of the table.

In the Chamber of Light, the room that devours itself, the sacred two of the air, and the sacred four of the almond eyes, and the sacred six in black armor shall unite beneath the sacred seven. And the light of the sacred seven will shine upon the head that is whole and the heart that is awake and the eyes that weep.

Olly had been staring at the riddle for over half an hour, but no matter how hard she concentrated, the words refused to mean anything to her. She pushed her notepad away and sighed as she munched on an apple. "This is giving me a headache," she said. "Let's face it — we're never going to work this out, even if we sit here for a million years!"
~~~~

Josh looked up at her. He was smiling.

"What's funny?" she asked.

"You are," he said. He tapped his pen on his pad. "Look."

Olly looked. Josh had drawn the rough shape of a snake, curled around into a ring with its tail in its mouth.

"Recognize that?" Josh asked.

"Yes," Olly replied. "It's like that symbol Dad showed us in the tomb."

"And do you remember what he called it?" Josh continued, grinning. "He said it was a picture of the snake that *devours* itself — an ancient symbol of eternity."

Olly leaned forward, interested now. "So, a snake that devours itself is a snake eating its own tail," she said. "But how does a room eat its own tail? It doesn't make sense."

Josh traced his pen around the snake shape. "See? It's a circle," he said. "I'm willing to bet that 'the room that devours itself' is a circular room."

"Josh, sometimes you're almost brilliant!" Olly declared. "That has to be it. You've solved the first part of the riddle. At this rate, we'll have the whole thing worked out by dinnertime! I can't wait to tell Dad."

"You can't wait to tell your dad what?" Mrs. Beckmann asked as she came to join them.

Excitedly, Olly and Josh explained their theory about the circular room. She was obviously impressed. "You're using your brains — I always approve of that — but I'm afraid you'll have to leave the rest for later," she said. "It's time for your lessons now."

Olly frowned. "But listen, Gran," she said firmly. "Seriously now, don't you think that solving this riddle is far more important than boring old lessons?"

"No," her gran replied. "I'll wait for you both in the trailer. Be there in five minutes."

And that was the end of the conversation.

~~~

Jonathan had arrived back from Cairo by the time Olly and Josh emerged from their lessons. The Elephantine Stone had been successfully deposited in the museum — well out of reach of any other would-be thieves. And Jonathan had some additional news. "We're to expect a special guest," he said. "She's in Italy right now, attending some film festival, but she'll be flying in to see us sometime tomorrow."

"Mom!" Josh shouted in delight.

Jonathan nodded, smiling. "She called me on my
~~~

cell phone while I was driving back." He winked at Olly. "Things are going to be pretty lively around here for a while," he said. "You know what these Hollywood stars are like!"

A huge grin spread over Olly's face. If there was one thing that would make this Egyptian adventure perfect, it was a visit from Josh and Jonathan's movie star mother, Natasha. As much as she loved the secrets of the sand and tombs, she would happily take a break for some Hollywood glamor. She couldn't wait.

~~~~~

Josh and Olly were up early the next morning. At breakfast, Olly bombarded Jonathan with questions about Natasha Welles's visit, but he wasn't able to tell her very much more. She would be arriving sometime that day, but she could only stay for a few hours — she was needed back in Rome to start shooting her new movie, a thriller called *Cat's Cradle*.

"She'll probably want a guided tour of the tomb," Josh said. He looked at Professor Christie. "Would that be OK?"

"It would be my pleasure," replied the professor.

"I've got an idea for her next movie," Olly said. "It could be set in ancient Egypt, and she could play
~~~~~

the female pharaoh, Nefertiti. She was supposed to be the most beautiful woman in the whole world at the time."

Mohammed arrived and made a low bow. "Excuse me, Professor, but I need your guidance on the clearing of the next chamber."

"Of course, I'll be right there." The professor drained his coffee cup and stood up. "Come on, Jonathan. We've a busy day ahead of us."

They hurried off with Mohammed, and Mrs. Beckmann started to clear the table. "You and Josh can help me with this," she said to Olly. "And it's Saturday today — laundry day — so I want all your dirty clothes in the basket."

Once their chores had been completed, Olly and Josh found themselves a good vantage point from which to watch the road. They were both impatient for the arrival of Josh's mother. Olly knew visits from Josh's mom were more like those from an eccentric aunt. Josh and Jonathan never knew when she'd decide to drop in, but they could always count on her having great stories to share.

"What's that noise?" Olly asked, after half an hour had passed without the sighting of a single car on the road.

Josh listened. It was a strange sound — a kind of

distant throbbing. He stood up, shading his eyes to peer into the distance. He saw a dark pinpoint in the sky and grinned. "It's a helicopter," he announced, with a laugh. "Mom's arriving in a helicopter!"

The arrival of the helicopter at the archaeological dig caused a major stir. Word had already gotten around the camp that a Hollywood movie star was coming, and the diggers threw down their tools and crowded around as soon as the rotors stopped spinning, all of them eager to catch a glimpse of the celebrity.

Natasha Welles stepped down from the helicopter, smiling and waving — every inch the movie star. Olly gazed at her in awe. Somehow Josh's mother always managed to look as if she was on a movie set — even now, when she was only dressed in jeans and a simple white blouse, with her long auburn hair tumbling loose down her back.

Josh and Olly pushed forward through the crowds as a second figure appeared at the door of the helicopter. "She brought Ethan with her," Josh remarked.

"Oh, is that bad?" Olly asked, recognizing that Ethan was the name of Natasha's latest boyfriend.

"No, Ethan's great," Josh replied happily. He

reached the front of the crowd and his mother opened her arms to greet him.

Olly knew about Ethan — anyone who read magazines, or watched TV, knew about Ethan Cain. He was a handsome, self-made millionaire who had earned a fortune in computer software. He now traveled the world as a modern-day adventurer. His name had been linked with Natasha Welles for several months now. There was even talk of a wedding, although both celebrities denied making long-term plans. Ethan was also dressed casually in a shirt and jeans. When no one else emerged from the helicopter, Olly realized that Ethan must have been the pilot. If any guy was cool enough for Josh's mom, Olly thought Ethan Cain just might be the one.

Natasha shook hands and gave autographs and made her way gradually through the crowd, her arm around Josh's shoulders. Jonathan was waiting for her by the trailers. They hugged and Jonathan shook Ethan's hand.

"Trust you to make a spectacular entrance," Jonathan said to his mother.

"You know me," Natasha replied with a laugh. She hugged Olly and Mrs. Beckmann. "It's lovely to see you all again," she said. She looked around. "And what an amazing place this is. I'm so glad Ethan persuaded me to take time off to come down here."

"There's lots to see," Olly said. "Do you want to visit the tomb? You'll never believe what's been going on — it all started when my dad found this old stone with —"

"For goodness sake, let Natasha catch her breath," said Mrs. Beckmann. "Come on into the trailer, I expect you could do with a rest and some lunch after your flight."

Natasha put an arm around Olly's shoulders. "Just let me get settled in, Olly," she said. "Then I want you to tell me everything that's happened." She gave Josh and Jonathan a knowing look. "My own children never tell me anything, so I'm relying on you to give me the full story."

~~~~

Olly and Josh had a great time over lunch. The professor missed it altogether, he was so wrapped up in his work, but Ethan was friendly and funny, talking of whitewater rafting in India and bungee jumping in New Zealand and scuba diving in Malaysia; his life seemed to be an endless series of exciting escapades. And Natasha clearly enjoyed being away from the pressures and expectations of
~~~~

her working life. She seemed happy and relaxed, and delighted Olly especially, by showing an interest in her adventures with Josh and chatting away like an old friend.

Both Natasha and Ethan were particularly fascinated by Josh and Olly's tale of the Elephantine Stone — its theft and spectacular recovery. Natasha laughed uproariously at Olly's description of her time inside the rolled-up carpet, and Ethan was riveted by the chaos caused when the ancient booby traps were triggered.

"And right now," Olly told them, "we're working on a riddle that my dad found in the tomb." She showed Ethan and Natasha the translation of the riddle, and Ethan seemed particularly intrigued by it.

"I think the first part means a circular room," Josh said, and explained his reasoning.

"Yes, I can follow that," Ethan agreed. "But what are the sacred two, four and six?"

"We're still working on that," Olly told him.

"It reminds me of the riddle of the Sphinx," Ethan said thoughtfully.

"Oh, yeah," Josh put in, looking at the others who sat at the table. "The one that initiates into the priesthood had to answer: What animal goes on four legs in the morning, two legs during the day, and three legs in the evening? The answer is 'human beings.' They crawl when they're babies — that's the morning of life. They walk upright as they grow up — that's the daytime of life. And they use a stick, like a third leg, when they're old — in the evening of life." He looked at the riddle. "So, do you think this could be similar?" he asked Ethan. "Two — four — six. Do you think they're supposed to be legs?"

"Yes, that's it!" Olly said. "A bird has two legs. Four legs would belong to some kind of land animal." She frowned. "And six legs could mean an insect."

"The Egyptians held the scarab beetle sacred," Jonathan pointed out. "That could be the answer. Two — four — six. Bird—animal — beetle."

"And seven?" Natasha asked.

Olly grinned. "An old beetle," she joked. "With a walking stick!"

Ethan laughed. "I don't think so."

Olly jumped up. "Me neither. But we've got most of it," she said to Josh. "We should go and tell Dad. He's going to be amazed!"

"And he might be able to help us make sense of the part about the sacred seven," Josh added. "We should ask him to take another look at the riddle on the wall of the Burial Chamber — I've got a feeling it might hold some more clues."

Chapter Nine: Moon-phase

Ethan Cain and Natasha Welles gazed up in awe at the beautiful paintings that covered the walls of Setiankhra's tomb.

"They're breathtaking," Natasha said, her voice hushed, her eyes wide. "I never realized they would be so colorful — or so detailed."

Olly smiled. "They *are* pretty impressive," she agreed. She was on her best behavior, in part because she was in the presence of a movie star, but also because she and Josh had been reminded that the tombs were not only sacred, but potentially dangerous. Ever since Olly set off the booby traps, the two friends had not been allowed in the tombs without an adult. She turned back to Jonathan and her father, who were examining the hieroglyphs of the riddle. "Have you found anything?" she asked.

They seemed to have been scrutinizing the glyphs and muttering quietly to each other for ages.

The professor stood up. "I can't see anything to suggest what the sacred seven might be," he said.

"There may be clues elsewhere, but it could take weeks to find them."

"That's too bad," Josh said. "I suppose we'll just have to keep working on it."

"But do you think we've got the rest right?" Olly asked her father. "Is 'the room that devours itself' a *circular* room?"

"It's a good theory," Professor Christie agreed. "Except for the fact that a circular room would be very unusual. The Egyptians seldom used curves in their architecture. A circular room would be quite unique."

Ethan stepped closer to the wall and looked at a hieroglyph to the left of the riddle.

"This bird image," he said, "it's a *benu*, isn't it?"

"Yes, a phoenix on a solar disc," Jonathan replied, coming up alongside him. "It's a frequent New Kingdom image."

"There are similar images in the tomb of Ramses the Fourth," Ethan murmured. "Have you worked out what it means in this context? Isn't that obelisk icon alongside it thought to be an embodiment of Osiris, the ruler of the Underworld?"

"Yes, it is," the professor confirmed. "I had no idea you were interested in Egyptology, Mr. Cain."

"Please, call me Ethan," he said. "I'm no expert,

Professor; I'm just an enthusiastic amateur. But I have a few interesting items that I've collected over the years, and I enjoy the research." He looked more closely. "Have the writings in this cartouche been translated yet?" He examined the ancient brushstrokes. "These symbols — they indicate *road*, don't they?"

Jonathan nodded. "Yes, the literal translation of this seems to be: *under me the backward road* — but we have no idea what it means."

"No." Ethan's voice was soft. "They certainly were a cryptic people."

Natasha laughed. "I know that tone, Ethan," she said. She looked at Olly, standing at her side. "His voice always gets that hazy sound just before he vanishes into one of his projects. It's a waste of time talking to him then — he's off in a world of his own."

Olly nodded. "Tell me about it," she sympathized. "Dad's just the same."

Natasha put an arm around Olly's shoulders. "Ethan, I'm going up top now," she said. "This place is incredible, but it's a little claustrophobic for my liking."

Ethan, Jonathan and the professor were over at the far wall, heads together, deep in conversation.

Natasha laughed. "See what I mean?" she said to Olly. "He's gone, already." She smiled at Josh. "Now then, do you two guys want to stay down here, or do you want to come with me and hear about my new movie?" For once, it was no contest. The three of them headed up the corridor to the surface.

"I want to hear all the latest Hollywood gossip," Olly said to Natasha.

"Well, I don't think there'll be time for *all* of it," she replied, laughing. "But I'll fill you in on all the juiciest parts." She looked over her shoulder. "Josh, are you coming?"

The three of them had been walking along together, but Josh had suddenly stopped to stare at the wall.

"What is it?" Olly asked, walking back. He was gazing at the depiction of the snake eating its own tail — the painting that had given him the idea of the circular room. He pointed to the stars that surrounded the snake. "Remember the professor mentioning these?" Josh asked.

"Yes," Olly replied. "They're the Pleiades. Except that the ancient Egyptians called them something else."

"The Krittikas," Josh told her. "Count them."

"One, two, three, four, five, six — oh!" Olly gasped. "*Seven*!"

"Seven sacred stars," Josh agreed. "*Seven* — just like the riddle says."

"We have to tell Dad," Olly said excitedly.

"We can tell him when he comes up," Josh said. "After all, the riddle only tells us what to look for once we're in the room that devours itself. Jonathan and your dad still have to figure out how to find that room."

Natasha was looking over their shoulders. "I'm sure they'll work it out," she said. "And Ethan might even be able to help. He was being rather modest down there — he's really quite an expert on this stuff. He has several hundred items on display back home, and a whole library full of reference books."

^^^^^

Time flew past for Olly and Josh as they sat with Olly's grandmother, drinking iced lemonade and listening to Natasha talk about her upcoming movie. It was midafternoon before Jonathan and Ethan emerged from the tomb and joined them under the umbrella.

"Professor Christie is still down there," Ethan said. "He's busy translating more of the writing."

"What have you people been doing?" Jonathan asked, pouring himself a glass of lemonade.

"Just chatting," Olly said casually. "Oh — and solving the last part of the riddle, as well."

Jonathan stared at her. "Excuse me?"

"We've figured out what the sacred seven are," Josh told him gleefully. "They're stars."

"The Krittikas!" Ethan said, leaning forward eagerly. "Of course! A sacred bird, a sacred animal, a sacred scarab and seven sacred stars." He laughed. "You two are amazing!"

"Aren't we, though?" Olly said with a grin. It wasn't every day that they received a compliment from the likes of Ethan Cain. She looked at Jonathan. "Now all you and Dad have to do is find that room."

"Easier said than done," Jonathan replied. "It could take six months to translate all the writings down there."

"But the clues must be there," Ethan said.

"I'm sure they are," Jonathan agreed. "Every aspect of the burial of a pharaoh had to be covered by protective spells — and every spell had to be written out in full. If the Tears of Isis were put in the tomb for safekeeping, then spells would have been placed around them to protect them from desecration."

"You mean from tomb robbers?" Josh asked.

Jonathan nodded. "But the spells weren't simply there to keep unwanted humans out," he said. "They were also there to stave off supernatural danger. The mythical world of the Egyptians was a dodgy place — if you didn't protect everything with very carefully worded and detailed spells, all kinds of bad things could happen. The pharaoh could lose his way on his journey to the next world, or his food could be poisoned by demons, or his heart could literally be stolen from him! Getting from this world to the next wasn't easy."

"I know you and Dad will find the Tears, eventually," Olly said. "And then they'll be put safely in a museum until we need them to open the Archives." She noticed a frown cross Ethan's face as she spoke, but it soon cleared.

"Which museum will you donate the Tears to, if they're found?" he asked Jonathan.

"The Egyptian Museum in Cairo," Jonathan replied. "Professor Bey, the Museum Director, has been kind enough to give us full access for research purposes."

"Natasha told me that you were on your way back from the museum when she called you," Ethan went on. "She said you put the Elephantine Stone there for safekeeping. I wish I could have seen it before it was locked away — it sounds fascinating."

"It's a shame I didn't call Jonathan before he handed it over," Natasha remarked. "I'm sure he'd have been happy to let you look at it." She turned to Jonathan. "Ethan was in Cairo, you know. That's where I met up with him to come down here. He's been there for several weeks."

"I've been looking into a real estate deal," Ethan said. "I'm thinking of opening a branch of my company there." He smiled. "But that's boring stuff. Has Natasha told you about some of the stunts she'll have to do in the new movie? They're pretty wild."

Josh looked impressed. "You didn't say you were going to do your own stunts, Mom! What kinds of stuff will you do?"

Natasha laughed. "Whatever they ask me to, I expect," she said. "Within reason, of course." And soon they were all enthralled by more tales of moviemaking.

The afternoon passed quickly, and all too soon for Josh and Olly, Natasha began to talk about the journey back to Rome.

"Can't you stay for just one night?" Josh asked. "It feels like you've only been here five minutes."

"We still have another hour or so," Ethan said.

He looked at Olly and Josh. "I've brought my camcorder with me, and I'd love to take some footage of the valley from the helicopter. I can't pilot the chopper and make a movie at the same time — would you two be interested in coming up with me to shoot some film?"

"Oh, yeah!" Josh said. "I can handle the camera."

"And I could do the commentary," Olly put in quickly.

Ethan smiled. "That's fine with me," he said.

Jonathan stayed with Natasha and Olly's gran, while Ethan led the two friends to the helicopter.

Once Josh and Olly were safely strapped in the back, Ethan climbed into the pilot's seat up front. Josh took command of the camcorder as Ethan gunned the engine. The noise rose to a steady, throbbing roar as the rotors began to turn — slowly and heavily at first, then faster and faster until they were just a dark blur.

Josh lifted the camera to his eye and pointed it out of the window to take some footage as the helicopter rose into the air.

"Whee-oo!" Josh whistled, as the land dropped quickly away below them. "This is great! I'm going to have to ask Mom to buy me one of these for my birthday."

"Which?" Olly asked. "The camcorder or the helicopter?"

"Both!" Josh replied laughing.

"Are you guys OK back there?" Ethan called.

"We're fine," Olly shouted back.

The helicopter circled and the landscape stretched out beneath them like a 3-D map. The mountains flung long shadows across the rugged terrain in the early evening sunshine and the Nile sparkled like a thread of silver. The little riverboats with their triangular sails lay on the water like resting butterflies. Olly spied New Gurna, nestling among green fields, and across the river, small and remote, she made out the broken temples and narrow streets of Luxor.

Ethan banked the helicopter and turned to the south, following the line of the valley. Olly leaned close over Josh's shoulder to call out the names of the tombs as they flew over them.

"That one to the right — point the camera over there, Josh — that's Ramses the Fourth's tomb, and right ahead of us and to the left is the tomb of the sons of Ramses the Second. It's called KV5, and it's where Kent Weeks found a whole bunch of secret chambers," Olly said.

"Just like what we'll probably find in Setiankhra's tomb," Josh added.

"And to the right is the tomb of Ramses the Second," Olly continued. "And directly ahead of us is the tomb of Tutankhamen."

The helicopter swept the length of the rugged valley, turning this way and that so that Josh could get clear shots of all the tomb entrances that dotted the craggy hills. The last tomb, deep in the shadow of overhanging cliffs, belonged to Tutmoses III.

Finally, Ethan swung the helicopter around and they headed north, back toward the excavation site.

"So, what turned you on to Egyptology, Ethan?" Josh asked.

"I suppose it was the remoteness and the grandeur of it," he replied. "And the epic scale of it all — the complexity of their civilization." A longing tone came into his voice. "They were a great people. Imagine if you could go back there to watch the pyramids being built — to learn all their lost secrets firsthand."

"Someone should invent a time-travel machine," Josh said.

"Yes," Ethan agreed. "Someone should."

The helicopter started to descend. "And so," Olly said, leaning over Josh's shoulder again, "we return to the newly discovered tomb of Setiankhra.

Inside, even as I speak, the famous British archaeologist, Professor Kenneth Christie, and his assistant, Jonathan Welles, are working to decipher the cryptic clues left by the ancient people of this land, and to find their way to the circular chamber that houses the Tears of Isis. Pictures supplied courtesy of Josh Welles. Your captain for this flight was Mr. Ethan Cain. And this is Olivia Christie, signing off. Thank you for your attention."

Olly noticed Josh roll his eyes at her, obviously thinking that her voice-over was a little much. She couldn't help but think that Josh lacked his mom's flair for the dramatic. Josh lowered the camcorder as Ethan brought the helicopter in to land, amid billowing clouds of dust.

"That was great," Ethan declared. "I loved the voice-over, Olly. Let's hope Josh got some good footage to complement it."

"I'm sure I did," said Josh. "It'd be pretty hard not to around here.

They clambered out of the aircraft and began to make their way back toward the trailers, where Olly's grandmother and Natasha were still chatting.

"I just want to check that everything's OK for the flight back to Cairo," Ethan called to the two friends. "You go ahead, I'll only be a few minutes."

Olly turned and nodded, but as she looked back at the helicopter, something caught her eye. Behind the door to the fuselage, a logo was painted on the side of the aircraft. It was a silver oval containing a silver crescent moon in one side and a silver full moon in the other. Beneath the logo, Olly read the word "Moon-phase."

"What's up?" Josh asked. He had stopped to wait for his friend.

Olly pointed at the logo. "Moon-phase," she said.

"That's right," Josh agreed. "I think it's a part of Ethan's computer firm. So what?" His eyes widened suddenly. "Oh! You're not thinking of that e-mail on Mohammed's laptop,are you?"

Olly nodded — momentarily speechless with surprise. The e-mail had said *ec@moon-phase.net. Could the "ec" have stood for Ethan Cain?* Olly wondered.

Ethan Cain at Moon-phase?

Chapter Ten: The Hidden Door

Olly and Josh stared at each other. Olly felt as if the world had suddenly turned upside down and inside out. She couldn't be absolutely certain that the e-mails from moon-phase.net had been sent by Ethan, but if they weren't, it was an extraordinary coincidence. *But why would Ethan Cain be sending e-mails to Mohammed?* Olly wondered. How would they even know each other? And, more to the point, exactly what kind of business venture would they be involved in together?

She looked again at the silver logo on the helicopter, and then back at Josh. "We shouldn't say anything," she murmured to him as they drew near the trailers. "Not till we've had time to think about this."

Josh nodded.

"I'll think of an excuse so we can get a few minutes on our own," Olly whispered. Then she waved at Natasha, Jonathan, and her gran, who were still sitting around the table outside. "That was a great trip!" she called as she and Josh walked over.

"Ethan's just checking out the helicopter," Josh said.

Natasha sighed. "Then we'll probably be on our way soon. What a pity. I'm having such a lovely time."

"That voice-over was thirsty work," Olly said. "I'm going to get myself a drink. Would anyone else like one?"

"Just bring a jug of water out, please," said Audrey Beckmann. "And some fresh glasses."

"I'll give you a hand," Josh offered, and the two friends hurried inside together.

As soon as the door closed behind them, Olly turned to Josh. "What on earth is going on around here?" she asked. "Is everyone in the world trying to get their hands on the Elephantine Stone? Even Ethan?"

Josh opened the fridge and took out a large bottle of mineral water. "It could all be perfectly innocent," he said.

"Hmm," Olly murmured dubiously. "A coincidence that Mohammed and that American thug have the same tattoo? A coincidence that part of Ethan's company is called Moon-phase, and that Mohammed is getting e-mails from someone at moon-phase dot net? A *coincidence* that all three of them happen to be in the same place at the same time?" She frowned. "I don't think so!"

"But even if you're right about the e-mail, Ethan might be doing some perfectly ordinary business with Mohammed," Josh suggested. "After all, Mohammed's an archaeology student, and Ethan's interested in archaeology."

Olly shook her head. "In which case, why hasn't Ethan mentioned that he knows Mohammed?" she asked. "Do you want to know what I think? I think Ethan's got something to do with the Elephantine Stone being stolen."

Josh shook his head. "He wouldn't do something like that," he protested. "He's a millionaire. If he wants something, he can just buy it. He doesn't have to steal stuff."

"He can't buy stuff that isn't for sale," Olly pointed out. "The Elephantine Stone *definitely* isn't for sale. And I just remembered something; Carter said he had a buyer lined up for the stone in Cairo. And Ethan has been in Cairo for the past few weeks, hasn't he?"

Josh stared at her. "You think Ethan was the *buyer*?" he gasped.

Olly nodded as a pattern began to form in her mind. "Maybe Mohammed and Carter were both working for Ethan," she breathed. "Mohammed's job was to steal the stone and hand it over to Carter. Then Carter was supposed to take it to Cairo and give it to Ethan. But the plan fell apart when *we* overheard Carter's plans and got the stone back!"

"That might have been why Ethan suggested to Mom that they come and visit us down here," Josh added. "Maybe he had an ulterior motive." Then he shook his head. "But Ethan seems like a really great guy. Besides, there are lots of artifacts around. Why would he want to steal this one?"

"I don't know. Maybe he wants things he can't have," Olly said grimly. "Or, maybe he wants the stone for the same reason we do."

"To help find the Tears of Isis?" Josh questioned. "But he had never heard of the Tears before we told him." Olly remembered Ethan's reaction to their explanation of the talismans. "He could just be a good actor," Olly suggested. "He's dating one."

Josh gazed at her, temporarily at a loss for words. "Even if you're right," he said at last, "we can't just go and tell everyone. They'll think we're out of our minds. Mom really likes Ethan. She's never going to believe he was involved in stealing the stone."

"True," Olly agreed thoughtfully. "And if we do say anything, Ethan and Mohammed will just deny it and we'll end up looking like idiots." Her forehead creased in concentration. "Maybe we're just jumping to conclusions," she said. "After all, Ethan knew the stone was safely locked away in Cairo before he came here. Your mom told him, remember? Besides, they're getting ready to leave now," she added. "If he was hoping to find the Tears, he'd need to stay here longer than one single day."

"Yes, but —" Whatever Josh had been intending to say was interrupted by the sound of the trailer door being opened from the outside.

Ethan appeared in the doorway. "I'll have some water, please, guys," he said. "Although I could use something a little stronger!"

Olly hastily poured the mineral water into a jug, while Josh got out the glasses. "Is there a problem?" she asked.

Ethan nodded. "There's a fault with the chopper's engine," he said. "We were lucky it didn't show till we were back on the ground. I'm going to have to send for a replacement part." He smiled ruefully. "It looks like we're going to be imposing on your hospitality a little longer than expected. Natasha is going to make some calls and reorganize her schedule. Jonathan will drive her back to Cairo in the morning, but I'll be staying here till the engine part arrives. But hey, every cloud has a silver lining; it'll give me more time to explore the tomb." He gave them a friendly wink. "You never know, I might even be able to help the professor find the room that devours itself."

He took the jug of water from Olly's hands and left the trailer.

Olly looked at Josh. "I bet there's nothing wrong with the helicopter," she hissed. "It's just an excuse for him to stay longer." Her eyes narrowed determinedly. "We're going to have to watch him every minute, day and night."

Josh nodded. "You're right. Poor Mom," he said. "She really likes him."

"Well, he's a rat," Olly said firmly. "And we're going to do everything we can to *prove* that he's a rat!"

~~~~

It was early evening, and long shadows were reaching out across the valley. The sun had dipped behind the western cliffs, but the sky was still bright. There were another two hours till dusk.

Olly and Josh were sitting at the table with Olly's grandmother, Josh's mother, and Ethan Cain. Natasha had just finished a call to her agent in Hollywood. She flipped her cell phone shut. "Judy
~~~~

is going to see that everything is reorganized for me," she told them. "If Jonathan and I head off early in the morning, I should still be able to catch the midafternoon plane from Cairo to Rome." She smiled at Olly. "Meanwhile, you can tell me more about that movie idea you have for me. Who would I be playing?"

"Nefertiti," Olly told her. "She was a really beautiful female pharaoh."

"If you're going to talk movies, I think I'll go and stretch my legs," Ethan said. He got up. "I'd like to see how Jonathan and the professor are getting along in the tomb."

The diggers were only employed for a half day on Saturday, but Olly's father and his assistant had decided to do some more exploring on their own. There was plenty of work to be done in Setiankhra's tomb that didn't require hired laborers.

Olly and Josh watched Ethan as he strolled past the trailers and turned out of sight at the end of the row. Josh wanted to stay and talk more with his mom, but his suspicion got the best of him.

"I think I'll go for a walk, too," Josh said, standing up.

"Me, too," Olly added.

Natasha gazed at them with a crooked smile.

"Everyone's abandoning me," she wailed. "Was it something I said?"

"Don't mind them," Audrey Beckmann commented. "They can't keep still for five minutes." She looked at the two friends. "Don't lose track of the time," she said. "I'll be starting dinner in an hour or so. I want you back here, washed, and ready to eat by eight."

"OK," Olly agreed. She smiled at Natasha. "We can talk about the movie over dinner. I've had some great ideas."

"I'll look forward to that," Natasha replied.

Josh and Olly wandered off after Ethan. "We can't just follow him," Josh whispered to Olly. "He'll see us."

"I know," Olly whispered back. "This way." Josh followed, and in moments they were peering from between the trailers.

"There he is," Olly whispered.

Ethan was heading toward the tomb entrance.

"Maybe he really *is* just going to see how Jonathan and your dad are getting along," Josh suggested.

Olly wasn't so sure. "Wait!" she hissed. Halfway to the tomb, Ethan gave a quick glance over his shoulder and then turned and strode briskly in the opposite direction — away from the tomb and toward the campsite.

"Got him!" Olly whispered sharply. "I'll give you two guesses who he's going to see."

The friends followed Ethan carefully, keeping low and sticking to the shadows as much as possible. As a result he got way ahead of them, but at least he didn't realize he was being tracked.

He rounded the shoulder of rock and disappeared from sight. Josh and Olly raced after him, scrambling up the side of the rocky outcrop.

"Keep your head down," Josh warned as they neared the crest of the ridge. They both peered cautiously over the top, and Olly let out a soft hiss of satisfaction.

Ethan Cain was only a few yards away from them, and Mohammed was with him. The two men were speaking together in low voices. The urgent murmurings drifted up to the friends, but neither of them could pick out any actual words that were being said. However, one thing was very clear from the tone of the men's voices and the way they were behaving: The two men knew each other and had far more pressing issues to discuss than the weather.

Their conversation lasted only a minute or so.

Mohammed gestured back the way Ethan had come, Ethan nodded sharply, and the two men turned and headed back together.

Olly and Josh flattened themselves against the rocks. They were well above the men, and unless either of them happened to glance upward, there was a good chance that the two friends wouldn't be spotted.

Olly watched as Ethan and Mohammed passed them and made their way toward the tomb. Mohammed was carrying a large flashlight.

"What do you think they're up to?" Josh whispered.

"No good, that's for sure," Olly replied. "Let's go."

They kept their distance as they trailed their quarry. The men were walking quickly, both of them looking around every now and then, as if to check that they weren't being observed. Olly and Josh's pursuit consisted of wild dashes from one point of cover to the next. It wasn't long before the men were a long way ahead of them, but they didn't dare draw any closer for fear of being seen.

Olly watched from the shadows of a long, low rock as Mohammed and Ethan entered the tomb of Setiankhra. "I wish we could have heard what they were talking about," she said. "What if they're just going down there to see how Dad and Jonathan are doing? That won't prove anything!"

"There's only one way to find out," Josh said. "Come on." He ran the last twenty yards to the tomb with Olly close behind. The entrance showed up clearly, a flare of electric light in the gathering dusk. "Slowly now," Josh murmured.

Olly nodded, knowing they were going against orders by entering the excavation on their own.

They stepped into the tomb, moving as quietly as possible, both of them listening intently for any telltale sounds of the two men. Silently, they crept across the wooden bridge and down the second corridor. As they neared the bottom, they heard voices.

Olly paused, her heart pounding.

Josh looked at her and put his finger to his lips. They pressed against the wall and edged a little closer to the entrance of the Burial Chamber.

"They've found it!" It was Ethan's voice, quiet but excited.

"They must have gone through," Mohammed said.

Olly came to the entranceway and peered around the corner of the chamber. There was no sign of Jonathan, or her father, but she could plainly see Ethan and Mohammed. The two men were standing together at the far end of the shadowy room. But it was something else that completely took her breath away.

Where the wall of the chamber previously had been smooth and flat, there was now a square opening, about three feet wide and slightly more than three feet tall. It was just below the place where the professor had pointed out the hieroglyphics that mentioned the sacred protector Nuit.

Olly's heart pounded. Her father and Jonathan had somehow found the hidden doorway! As Mohammed had said, they must have gone through to explore because there was no sign of them on this side of the doorway. How could they resist?

"I had no idea they were so close to finding the hidden entrance," Ethan remarked. "We must follow them."

Mohammed gripped Ethan's arm as the older man ducked to go through the door. His voice was suddenly low and urgent. "Look!" he said, pointing to the writings over the door. "Do you see the hieroglyphs?"

"I don't have time to translate," Ethan snapped. "What do they say?"

Mohammed moved closer to the wall. Something in his voice sent shivers up Olly's spine as he translated. "*This shall be the gift of Nuit to thee, traveler on the backward road. Thou shalt not die. Thou shalt move through all the ages. Thou shalt have one foot in the future and one foot in the past. Deathless traveler, thou shalt live for a hundred million years.*"

Ethan let out a slow, triumphant breath. "Ahhhh!" He gripped Mohammed's shoulder. "Just as I'd hoped!"

But Mohammed backed away from the wall, his eyes uneasy. "I will not go through there," he said. "The danger is too great. Night is coming, and a powerful moon is rising. This is not the time to desecrate a tomb protected by Nuit." He shivered, staring around warily. "I feel her presence all around me in this place," he muttered. Then he turned and looked intently at Ethan. "There's still time to give this up — to go away from here and forget."

Ethan moved purposefully toward him. "Forget?" he murmured. "Forget something I've been searching for all my life? I don't think so. I have as much right to it as anyone."

"Then you must travel the road alone," Mohammed told him. "I will have nothing more to do with it." He turned and walked out of the chamber. He rushed right past Olly and Josh, and headed up the corridor to the surface.

Olly flinched away, treading on Josh's feet as she tried to keep out of Mohammed's sight. Josh caught her hand and pulled her quickly into one of the side chambers.

"I'm going in," they heard Ethan snarl at Mohammed. "And I need you to come with me."

Mohammed paused just beyond the entrance to the side chamber. "No, not tonight," he said, defiant. "It isn't safe." The writings on the wall had clearly unnerved him.

Olly saw Ethan stride after Mohammed. She sidled to the entrance of the chamber and peered out.

Ethan had caught up with Mohammed just a little farther up the passage. "Think about what we might find!" he was saying, his voice urgent and persuasive. "Are you really willing to give up the chance to claim the Tears of Isis?"

The Egyptian's footsteps faltered. Ethan's words had obviously had an effect on him. He turned back uncertainly. And then his eyes locked on Olly!

Ethan whirled around, searching the tomb. When he caught sight of Olly, he lunged.

"Josh! Time to get out of here!" Olly yelled, running away from Ethan and down into the Burial

Chamber. Josh raced after her, with both Ethan and Mohammed close on his tail.

The friends tumbled into the stone chamber as an angry shout from Ethan echoed off the walls behind them. They were trapped — there was no way out. No way but one!

Olly caught hold of Josh's sleeve and dragged him through the darkened doorway in the chamber's wall. "Help me!" she gasped. And, together, she and Josh heaved the heavy stone doorway closed, just as Ethan hurled himself toward it.

In spite of Ethan's momentum, the door thudded shut, plunging Olly and Josh into deep, impenetrable darkness.

Chapter Eleven: Secrets of the Tomb

A thin beam of bright light cut suddenly through the darkness. Josh had pulled a small flashlight from his pocket. The light illuminated a gray stone wall and a floor strewn with rubble. They were in a narrow corridor that stretched away to the left and right, parallel to the Burial Chamber.

"We need to find Dad," Olly said.

Josh raked the beam of light along the featureless corridor in both directions. "Which way?" he asked.

They heard the grinding sound of stone grating on stone. Josh aimed the flashlight at the doorway. It was being pushed open from the outside.

Olly didn't wait to think. "This way!" she said, running to the left.

Josh followed, taking a quick look over his shoulder as he ran. He saw a crack of light in the wall — Ethan and Mohammed would soon have the door open again.

Olly was in the lead. "Give me the flashlight!" she gasped. Josh handed it over. Olly grazed one hand along the wall as the thin white beam stretched out ahead of them, lighting up the rough floor and the narrow gray walls.

A black slit appeared in the wall to their right. They ran past it. There was another, and another — dark passageways leading off at right angles to the main corridor.

A flare of light behind them threw their shadows forward. They were caught in the bright beam of a powerful flashlight. Ethan and Mohammed were chasing them along the corridor.

Olly caught hold of Josh's arm and pulled him into one of the side passages. This new corridor was exactly the same as the other: a straight, gray tunnel, a little more than shoulder-width, and around six feet high.

But then they came to something different: a small chamber. Olly shined the flashlight around. The walls were covered in intricate paintings. Animal-headed figures sat in profile on chairs, watching as a jackal-headed figure — which Olly recognized as Anubis — weighed a human heart against a feather on a set of simple scales. The crocodile-headed god, Thoth, waited nearby. Olly knew his task: to gobble down any hearts that failed the test and were heavy with misdeeds. Rows of hieroglyphs filled the spaces between the paintings.

"Wow!" Olly breathed.

"No time for 'wow'," Josh panted. "Which way out?" Five identical tunnels led off in every direction, like spokes from the hub of a wheel.

"Beats me," Olly gasped. She tried to go over their route in her head. Left from the doorway, then a right had brought them here. If they wanted to work their way back around to the doorway in the Burial Chamber, she figured they should go right and right again. With some luck, that would take them full circle.

Olly flashed the light into the tunnel that led off to the right. "This one!" she said.

They ran along the stone passage deeper and deeper into the heart of the mountains. Olly kept looking for a corridor that went to the right, but there was none, so they kept running. Soon, she noticed that the walls here were inlaid with green jasper. And painted cobras, with gleaming jeweled eyes, reared up the sides of the corridor.

The friends came to a sharp bend. The wall ahead was covered in a huge painting of Osiris, god of the Underworld, holding a crook and flail. His wife, Isis, stood behind him, and ahead of them were the four sons of Horus.

In spite of the fear of pursuit, Olly had to be

dragged away from the wall painting. She had spent all her life learning about ancient Egypt from her father — and now she was seeing ancient masterpieces that had lain hidden for thousands of years. It felt to Olly as if they were running through a kaleidoscope of Egyptian mythology, going ever deeper into a dead world that their presence was bringing back to life.

"We're going down," Josh commented.

"I know," Olly replied. The tunnel had been sloping for some way now. Olly didn't like to think of how far under the surface they must be. "Not again!" she gasped.

They had come to another chamber with six exits leading out of it. Here the paintings depicted green boats sailing across an azure sky. Seated in the largest boat was a man with a scarab for a head. A lion lay — sphinxlike — shaded by papyrus plants that were entwined with cobras.

Again, Olly chose the tunnel to the right. If her mental picture of the place was accurate, she thought, they should now be heading back to the main part of the tomb. There was only one problem: How deep under the ground were they now? The passage ran level for some time, but then it dipped alarmingly, shooting down like a ramp into a well of darkness.

Olly pointed the flashlight down, but the tunnel fell away beyond the beam. "This can't be right," she panted. "We're too deep. We should go back and find a passageway that heads upward."

Josh stared back up the tunnel. "Can I have the flashlight?" he asked.

Olly handed it to him. He sent the beam skidding back the way they had come. A thousand almond-shaped eyes glittered at them from the walls. "Listen!" Josh said.

Olly held her breath and strained her ears.

"Hear it?" he asked.

She nodded. It was distant, but unmistakable: the sound of feet pounding on stone, echoing down through the corridors and chambers. Ethan and Mohammed were still in pursuit.

"We can't go back," Josh said. "We might run straight into them."

"Where are Jonathan and Dad?" Olly wailed.

"They must have gone another way," Josh said. "There were lots of side tunnels. They could be anywhere!"

"Great!" Olly took a deep breath, exasperated. "We'd better keep going then," she decided.

They hurried on, side by side, down the slope. The corridor tilted as steeply as a child's slide, making it difficult for Josh and Olly to keep on their feet. Then Olly brought her heel down on a piece of loose stone that skidded away beneath her. She slipped and fell into Josh, and soon they were both sliding down the shaft, the flashlight skimming the walls and ceiling as they plunged downward.

Their fall was halted by a bank of loose, dry sand and rubble. They tumbled into it, breathless and bruised. It was a few moments before Olly could catch her breath enough to speak. "Are you OK?" she asked.

"I think so." Josh groaned, sitting up. Sand cascaded off his clothes. He shined the flashlight beam around them. "Look at that." He pointed the beam at the top of the bank of sand and stones where it reached the ceiling of the passage. The roof had fallen in and the heaped sand and rubble was the result of the collapse. "It's completely blocked!" Josh said. "We'll never get through. And listen . . ."

Again, they could hear the telltale sounds of pursuit. And now, mixed in with the echoing footfalls, they could also hear voices, weirdly distorted, drifting down the long slope toward them.

"Well, we can't go back," Olly said. "Shine the light here." Josh turned the flashlight back onto the sand and rubble. Olly crawled up to where the debris met the roof and began to dig, scooping out the sand and throwing the lumps of stone down behind her.

"What are you doing?" Josh asked.

"What does it look like?"

"But the tunnel could be blocked for another twenty yards!" Josh pointed out.

Olly ignored him. She was working hard, shoveling the sand away with both hands.

Josh shook his head. "This is crazy," he sighed. But he scrambled up the slope and joined Olly, holding the flashlight under his chin and using his hands to dig away the sand and rock.

The pair worked in dogged silence for some minutes. Sweat was pouring off them onto the sand and they were both gasping for breath. They had moved forward about three feet, and then, quite suddenly, Olly wrenched a lump of stone away and found a hole. They had reached the place where the roof had caved in.

They renewed their efforts, revealing a broken-edged gap that expanded to the full width of the roof. Olly took the flashlight and squirmed up through the hole. "It goes up about six feet," she called down to Josh. "I can see exits to either side — and a roof. I think it's another passage running right above this one!"

They cleared away more debris and soon stood side by side in the hole.

"Cup your hands," Olly said. "Help me climb up."

Half a minute later, the two friends were standing in the higher tunnel. Josh had the flashlight now. He pointed the beam to the right. "Uh-oh!" he said. This corridor ended in a flat stone wall, about twelve yards away. He turned the beam the other way and sighed with relief. The tunnel continued ahead for twenty yards or so, then there was a black square — an entrance or an exit.

The friends hurried on together, and stepped through the entrance. They found themselves standing on a platform of white stone slabs, flanked by life-sized shabti warriors made of shining quartz crystal. Josh moved the flashlight beam around the chamber they had entered. It was huge, the roof soaring up and away in a high arch of faintly glowing white rock. Olly saw that the walls were carved with bas-relief depictions of the soul's journey to the afterlife.

Two immense stone columns, decorated with carved palm fronds, held the roof up. At the base of each pillar sat a huge black statue — at least ten feet tall — of Osiris, the god who watched over the netherworld. Next to him sat a statue of his son,

Horus, with a falcon's head and eyes of gold and silver — to represent the sun and the full moon.

Behind these two majestic gods a vast chasm opened up, splitting the chamber in two.

"Can you believe this?" Olly murmured as she slowly crossed the chamber.

Josh didn't reply. He was gazing around in awe.

They walked together to the edge of the chasm. Josh pointed the flashlight at the far side. It was easily five yards away. The light also revealed a slender stone bridge spanning the gulf, just wide enough for a person to cross. There was no handrail or support. Beyond the bridge was another platform of white stones, and a dark, square gateway in the far wall of the chamber, also guarded by shabti warriors. Their green jeweled eyes glinted menacingly in the flashlight beam.

Josh stepped forward and shined the flashlight down into the chasm. Many feet below he saw a forest of sharpened stone spikes and, with a shudder, he noticed that human skeletons lay among them. He looked at Olly. "That's not a comforting sight," he said quietly.

Olly pursed her lips and stared at the thin, white stone bridge. "We can do it," she said. She glanced at Josh. "Do heights bother you?"

"Do they bother *you*?" he returned.

Olly shook her head.

"That's good, then," Josh said firmly. "I'll go first." Olly nodded and Josh stepped carefully out onto the bridge. He shined the light down at his feet. Olly swallowed hard, trying not to think about the spikes and skeletons below as she edged onto the bridge behind him. The stonework was narrow and smooth, but it looked safe.

Slowly they approached the middle of the bridge. "How are you doing?" Olly asked, surprised to find that her voice was shaking.

"It's easier than I expected," Josh replied. "And by the way, I *don't* like heights."

Olly smiled. "You're doing fine," she told him.

"Thanks," Josh said, glancing over his shoulder. But it was a bad move. Momentarily distracted, Josh stumbled. Olly reached forward to catch him as he tripped, but she missed. He fell hard. His fingers managed to catch the bridge, but the flashlight fell from his hand.

Olly watched in horror as it plummeted into the chasm.

Chapter Twelve: The Golden Doors

Josh heard a crack as the flashlight hit stone somewhere far below, and then the chamber was lost in utter blackness. He lay sprawled on the cold stone bridge, facedown, his heart hammering. His fingers gripped the edges of the bridge while his mind whirled. He had dropped the flashlight! They were lost and blind and one wrong move could send them plunging down to the deadly spikes below.

He felt Olly's hands on his legs and heard her voice. "Josh — are you OK?" she asked.

"Yes. You?" he answered.

"I'm fine," Olly replied. "But we need to get off this bridge." Josh knew she must be terrified, but her voice sounded calm. "I'm going to back up. We'll just have to hope Ethan and Mohammed find us. At least they've got a flashlight. We'll never get out of here without a light."

"No." Josh felt himself growing calmer. His brain was beginning to work again. "Stay where you are." He rose cautiously to his hands and knees and then sat back on his heels. He fumbled in his pockets until his fingers found the piece of candle and box of matches he carried with him.

His hands trembled as he opened the box and struck a match. The light flared and grew steady. Josh touched the match to the candlewick, which caught and burned brightly. He was pleased by how strong the flame was. Now he could see the ground at his feet — though the shadows hemmed him in on all sides.

He turned. Olly was staring at him, her eyes bright in the candlelight. "You carry a candle?" she asked incredulously.

Josh nodded. "Jonathan gave it to me. He always carries matches and a piece of candle in the tombs. Just in case."

"Smart," Olly said. "Remind me to thank him. Could we get off this bridge now?"

Very carefully, the pair made their way to the far side of the chasm. Josh felt an overwhelming sense of relief when he finally stepped off the narrow bridge. He lifted the candle to see the exit from the chamber and headed toward it. Olly followed, and the dark raced in behind her as though it was giving chase.

Beyond the exit the tunnel was no more than ten feet long. It opened into another chamber so huge that Josh and Olly couldn't see the far walls or the roof. On either side of the entrance stood massive obsidian statues, each with the head of a hawk.

"That's Horus," Olly remarked nervously as she gazed up into the god's fierce face. "The patron of the living pharaohs." The statue's black eyes stared out over Olly's head, its haughty gaze fixed eternally on the engulfing darkness. She touched the cold, shining stone of the statue. "When was the last time anyone saw this?" she murmured. "It must have been thousands of years ago."

Josh raised the candle. The walls that stretched away on either side of the entrance were covered with immense bas-relief sculptures, depicting mythical scenes of gods and men and animals. Their colors shone in the flickering candlelight — red and gold and green, blue and yellow and white — eventually disappearing into the darkness.

Awed by the vastness of the place, Josh and Olly moved farther into the room. And then they both gasped in wonder and disbelief, because piled around the towering pillars that supported the roof lay golden treasures! Plates and jeweled goblets, statuettes and swords, shields and bowls, all glittered and gleamed and threw back the candlelight.

Josh's head spun with the wonder of it all. He

felt small and insignificant among such wealth and beauty and grandeur. The light of the candle seemed a tiny flicker in that great lost hall of treasures.

"It's as if they're watching us," Olly said, her voice low with awe.

Josh turned and saw that she was referring to two great statues that had emerged from the gloom ahead of them. They *did* seem almost alive, he thought. As if at any moment a head would turn and a hand lift, creaking with the weight of years. It was scary, but it was wonderful at the same time.

They walked between them and found themselves in a colonnade of warrior statues, all facing inward. A wall appeared at the end of the guarded aisle. It was covered in richly colored paintings. This time, all the people and animals were facing to the right.

"It's like a kind of procession," Olly said, approaching the painting. "I wonder where they're all going."

The wall arced, and Olly followed the painted procession around the curve. "Josh?" Olly's voice was breathless with excitement. "This is a curved wall!"

"Yes, I noticed," Josh replied. He knew what Olly was thinking — the same thought had occurred to him. Did the wall form a circle? And if so, what lay inside?

The procession ended. Two women in white robes knelt at the feet of a tall figure with the head of a jackal — the god Anubis, who escorted souls on their journey to the Underworld. At his back was a mass of hieroglyphic writings. And beyond that was a pair of huge, closed doors, made of gleaming, beaten gold. Josh could see a tawny, rippled reflection of his own face in the shiny metal.

For some time, the friends just stood there, staring up at the golden doors, speechless with amazement, all thought of their pursuers forgotten. Olly was the first to break the silence. "I think this is it," she whispered reverently. "I think we've found the room from Nuit's riddle!"

Chapter Thirteen: The Chamber of Light

"How do we get in?" Olly whispered, staring up at the doors.

Josh held the candle closer, searching for a handle or a lever. There was nothing. He winced as the candle guttered and a rivulet of hot wax burned his fingers. He looked down anxiously. The candle was already half eaten away by the flame. It wouldn't be much longer before it became too short to hold. And then what? He had matches, but they were only good for a few seconds each. And once the matches were gone, the darkness would swallow them whole, and that would probably be the end of them. He decided not to share his thoughts with Olly.

She was moving back and forth, running her hands over the doors, as if hoping to find something invisible to the eye. She pushed against the doors. They didn't move. "There has to be a way to get them open," she said.

"Open sesame!" Josh intoned solemnly. Nothing happened.

"That's Arabian legend, not Egyptian," Olly said, dropping to her knees. "Give me some light."

Josh crouched beside her. She was at the join between the doors. Here, the stone floor had been hollowed out to make a small hole. Olly pushed her fingers in under the doors. "I can feel something," she said. "It's hard and sharp and—" There was a loud metallic click and Olly saw the doors shiver slightly. She stood up and pressed her hand against them. They swung smoothly inward.

Together, the two friends moved forward into the room, all thought of danger temporarily forgotten in astonishment and delight. The room was like the inside of a huge golden bell. The enclosing walls and the vaulting ceiling were made of panels of highly polished gold, which glowed dark yellow in the candle flame. The panels were etched all over with fine drawings and writings. Even the floor was gold.

Olly looked at Josh, her eyes shining. "How did the riddle go?"

Josh handed Olly the candle stub as he rummaged in his pocket, then unfolded the sheet of paper. "'In the Chamber of Light, the room that devours itself, the sacred two of the air, the sacred four of the almond eyes, and the sacred six in black armor shall unite beneath the sacred seven,'" Josh recited. "'And the light of the sacred seven will shine upon the head that is whole and the heart that is awake and the eyes that weep.'"

"OK, we think the two and the four and the six represent legs, and the seven are the Pleiades," Olly said. "But what does the rest mean?"

"I don't know, yet. But look!" Josh pointed across the room. On three slender gold bases stood three small gold sculptures. Olly and Josh walked toward them. One was an ibis — a tall, long-beaked, spindle-legged bird. Its wings were spread wide and its sinuous neck arched down and forward, supporting a flat golden plate which rested on its wing tips and head.

The next was a sitting cat, slender and elegant with a haughty, Abyssinian face. Between its ears was a strange kind of headpiece, almost like a crown, with a smooth, flattened top.

The last of the golden sculptures was a beetle with a golden dish on its back.

"Two legs, four legs, six legs," Olly said happily. "It's them. What about the seven?"

Josh shook his head. He began to circle the room, peering at the etched pictures as they flashed in the guttering light of his failing candle. The wax had burned down almost to his fingers now. It would only be a matter of minutes before he couldn't hold it anymore.

Something sparkled in the light. He held the candle closer. There was a pattern of white jewels set into the gold of the wall — seven white diamonds arranged in the same formation as the Pleiades! And about three feet below them was a small golden shelf. "Bring the statues over here," Josh called.

Olly lifted the heavy, golden cat off its base.

"No!" Josh directed. "The bird first."

Olly nodded and quickly exchanged the cat for the ibis.

Josh pointed and she rested it on the shelf.

"Now the cat."

Olly brought the cat over and placed it on the gold plate on the bird's head. Its base nestled perfectly on top of the plate. She ran back for the beetle. The sacred insect sat right on the cat's headpiece, the dish on its back in line with the lower stars in the arrangement of diamonds. "Now what?" she demanded.

"I don't know," Josh replied. "It looks as if something should fit into the dish on the beetle's back." He looked around the room. "Is there anything else?"

"I don't think so," Olly responded, also gazing around.

"What else do we have to do?" Josh asked. "Why hasn't anything happened?" He racked his brains. What had they missed? The three sacred animals had been united under the seven jewels. They had fit together perfectly. So why weren't the Tears of Isis revealed?

Olly gave a sharp hiss and whipped around to face the doors, which still stood open.

"What is it?" Josh asked.

Olly ran to the doors and peered out. "I can see a flashlight beam coming this way," she said. "It must be Ethan and Mohammed."

"Close the doors," Josh instructed.

Olly heaved against the doors and they swung closed with a clang.

Josh winced at the noise. "If they didn't know we were here before, they do now," he remarked.

"I couldn't help it," Olly snapped, leaning against the doors to hold them shut. "Get working on the riddle. I'll try and keep them out."

Josh stared at the seven jewels. "The light of the sacred seven," he muttered under his breath. "What light? What does it mean?"

Something hit the outside of the doors. The blow vibrated through Olly's back. She flexed her legs, digging her heels in. "Josh!"

Ethan and Mohammed obviously weren't bothering to look for the release mechanism — they had resorted to brute force.

"Try to find something to wedge the doors shut," Josh suggested, thinking furiously. He had only one goal: to solve the riddle before the two men burst in. For once, he wasn't thinking about what might happen afterward.

Boom! Another blow struck the doors.

Olly ran toward the slender base that had held the cat statue.

Boom! The doors shuddered.

"What light do they mean?" Josh yelled in frustration.

"Try the candle!" Olly shouted. "It's the only light we've got."

Josh looked at Olly and smiled. It was worth a try. He placed the small candle-end in the dish on the scarab's back and stepped away. The flame flickered. For a moment Josh thought it was going to go out. But then it grew stronger, flaring up with a heart as bright as sunlight.

The seven jewels caught the light from the swelling candle flame. They burned with a blinding intensity, their white light building and building as it reflected and rebounded from the polished surfaces of the golden room, until the whole chamber blazed like the sun.

This must be why it's called the Chamber of Light, Josh thought, shielding his eyes with his hand, as a beam of light leaped across the room from the seven jewels to strike a panel in the far wall. A rumbling noise filled the room. He watched in amazement as the golden wall panel slid back to reveal a recess. There was a statue in the secret alcove — the figure of Isis, made entirely of gold. Her hands were together, palms upward. And as the light touched them, it scattered into myriad different colors that bounced and rebounded off the walls, roof, and floor, in a dazzling rainbow of light.

At that instant, the doors flew open and Ethan Cain and Mohammed burst into the room. Ethan's eyes were bright and feverish as they focused on the statue. "Ah! The Tears of Isis!" he cried. "At last!"

The two men moved toward the statue of Isis, stumbling directly into the brilliant beam of light. Immediately, they fell back — blinded — trying to protect their eyes.

As Josh stood frozen in shock, staring at the two men, he saw a movement out of the corner of his eye. Olly held one of the golden bases in her hands. She swung it and, with both arms, threw it across the room. The heavy golden column spun through the air and struck Ethan on the shin. He let out a bellow of pain and crumpled to the floor, dragging Mohammed down with him. The Egyptian dropped the flashlight as he fell and it skidded across the floor toward Josh.

"Come on!" Olly yelled to Josh as she ran to the statue. In her open hands, Isis held a small, golden casket. The lid was open, and inside glittered two enormous, pear-shaped, blue sapphires. Olly snatched the casket up, and as she did so, the lid fell shut, instantly extinguishing the lights. A split second later, Josh's candle flickered and died. The only light now came from Mohammed's flashlight.

Josh ran forward and picked up the flashlight, then he and Olly skirted the two men and raced for the door.

"The Tears of Isis. At last?" Olly muttered to Ethan as she and Josh pushed the doors shut. "I don't think so!"

As the doors came together, Josh caught a last glimpse of Ethan through the crack. He was clambering to his feet, his face twisted with pain and anger. He shouted something, but the words were lost behind the clanging doors.

The friends ran, Josh in the lead with the powerful flashlight, Olly right behind him.

"We need to go back the same way we came!" Josh shouted.

"We'll never find it!" Olly yelled.

Josh realized she was right. The golden room was encircled with avenues of guardian statues. It would take them forever to find the original row and retrace their steps to the surface — even if they were able to remember the way.

They hurried on through the hall of treasures, until the beam of the flashlight hit a far wall and revealed a doorway. As they neared the exit tunnel, Olly paused for a moment and looked back over her shoulder.

"What's wrong?" Josh asked.

"Just making sure it's real," Olly said with a smile.

They emerged into a corridor that sloped gently upward. Josh and Olly could hear no sounds of pursuit, so they slowed to a brisk walk.

"This must lead somewhere important," Olly said hopefully after a while. "And we're going upward all the time — that's good news."

"How far do you think we've come?" Josh asked.

"I don't know," Olly replied, then stopped for a

moment, listening. She shook her head. "I can't hear anything back there," she said. She looked at Josh. "Once we're out, we're going to have to get someone to help us rescue those two. We can't leave them down there without any light."

Josh nodded. "But we have to get ourselves out first," he said. "Show me the Tears again."

Olly opened the casket and the sapphires sparkled in the flashlight beam.

"Aren't they fabulous?" Olly breathed.

"Amazing," Josh agreed. He grinned. "I can't wait to show them to Jonathan and your dad."

"Then we'd better get moving," Olly said. She shut the casket and the glorious blue light went out.

They walked on. Several minutes later, Josh saw something ahead of them. A small square of blacker darkness, some way in the distance. He began to walk more quickly. Olly kept up with him and soon they were both running. The square of darkness grew.

They burst out into a large square chamber. The floor was silted and scattered with debris, and the walls were covered in paintings and hieroglyphs. A flight of ten large stone steps led to the roof. The foot of the stairway was guarded by grim shabti warriors of black granite.

Josh shined the flashlight around the chamber. There didn't seem to be a way out.

"Those steps must be there for a reason," Olly said, staring up to where the steps met the ceiling of stone blocks. She moved toward the stairway.

"Watch where you walk," Josh warned her. "There might be traps."

Olly slowed down. "I'll be extra careful," she said. At the foot of the stairs she stopped and looked up. "It seems safe enough," she murmured and brought one foot down tentatively on the bottom step. She looked over her shoulder at Josh. "It's fine," she told him. But as she put her weight on the step, it slid downward a few inches with a grating sound. "Oh, please — no. Not another booby trap!" Olly breathed.

A low rumble sounded from above her head. Josh shined the flashlight upward. Sand was filtering down from between cracks in the stone roof. Loud grating and grinding sounds now filled the chamber. "Move!" Josh shouted.

Sand began to cascade down, with small stones that bounced on the steps and struck Olly on her head and shoulders. She threw herself backward as a large block came crashing down, striking the stairs and breaking them as it tumbled to the floor. In its wake, sand and rubble cascaded out of the rift in the ceiling.

Breathing in a mouthful of dust, Olly thought, *This is it. This is the Christie family curse, taking its turn on me, the firstborn girl.*

"Olly!" Josh shouted in panic. He heard her scream, but then she vanished from sight — suddenly hidden by the flood of debris that poured from the broken ceiling and rushed in a torrent down the steps.

Chapter Fourteen: The Tears of Isis

Dust billowed in thick gray clouds, clogging Olly's lungs and sending her reeling backward as the roof of the chamber fell in.

"Olly!" she heard Josh shout, but her mouth was thick with grit and she couldn't reply. She scrambled into a corner of the chamber and rolled herself into a protective ball as dirt and stones showered down over her. She expected to be crushed at any moment by a falling stone block.

But it didn't happen. The noise lessened and the surge of debris dwindled to a trickle of sand and pebbles. She took her arms away from her head and stared upward. At first she couldn't understand what she was seeing. It looked like dark blue velvet scattered with diamonds. *It must be another ceiling*, she thought, *above the chamber roof — painted to look like the night sky*.

A breath of air touched her cheek. Her vision cleared and the roof of stars suddenly leaped away into the far, far distance. She realized that she was gazing up at the sky — the *real* night sky!

"We did it!" she breathed. "We escaped!"

She looked across the chamber for Josh. The clouds of dust were thinning and she saw him pressed against the far wall, staring at her in shocked relief.

"I thought you were killed!" he said.

Olly grinned. "Not me," she replied. But she was only too aware of how lucky she had been. The booby trap had clearly been set to catch anyone climbing the stairs. The fact that she had thrown herself backward, away from the steps, had saved her life.

Josh came over to help Olly to her feet. Together, they climbed over the wreckage and scrambled up the stairs.

"Fresh air!" Olly said. "Can you smell it?"

"Yes," Josh replied with a happy sigh.

Earth and sand sloped up to ground level a few feet above their heads. It was late evening and a rare whisper of breeze came over the western mountains.

"I wonder where we are," Olly said.

The crater hole was several yards across. They began to climb out.

"Olivia! Josh! What on earth is going on? How did you get down there?" came a familiar voice from above.

"Gran?" Olly said in surprise. Her head came up

above ground level and she instantly saw where she and Josh had surfaced. They were in front of the trailers, not far from the table and chairs. Natasha Welles and Audrey Beckmann were gazing down into the chasm that had opened up almost under their feet.

"Josh!" Natasha gasped.

"I'm OK, Mom," Josh called.

Mrs. Beckmann stared into the hole. "What have you been up to?" she demanded as she helped Olly out. "You're not supposed to be in there by yourselves. You could have been killed! And if you've caused any damage down there your father will never forgive you."

Natasha offered a helping hand to Josh, looking at the two disheveled friends in astonished disbelief.

Olly grasped her gran's hands, her face glowing. "It's huge down there, Gran — bigger than you'd ever believe," Olly explained. "We found the room that devours itself. But Ethan and Mohammed were chasing us. They're still down there, and —"

"What are you talking about?" her grandmother interrupted. She frowned at Josh. "What is all this nonsense?"

"She's telling the truth," Josh said. "Ethan wants the Tears for himself." He looked at his mother.

"I'm sorry, Mom, but it's true. We need to find Jonathan and the professor."

Natasha looked completely bewildered. "Surely they're still down in the tomb," she said. She frowned at Josh. "I don't understand — what was that about Ethan?"

Olly impulsively gave her grandmother a hug. "We've got so much to tell you," she said. "But right now I have to find Dad." She drew back and pulled the golden casket out of her pocket. "You see, we've found the Tears of Isis!" And with that, she broke away from her gran and raced toward the main entrance of the tomb. Josh chased after her.

The two stunned women looked at one another for a moment, and then they, too, began to run toward the tomb of Setiankhra.

~~~

Olly and Josh tumbled into the Burial Chamber, just as Jonathan and Professor Christie were climbing out through the secret doorway.

"You're safe!" Olly exclaimed happily. "I was afraid they might have done something to you."

"Olly, marvelous news!" exclaimed the professor. "We've found the sarcophagus of Setiankhra!" He gestured toward the doorway. "It's in a chamber through there. It's the most wonderful thing!"
~~~

Jonathan looked at the two friends. "What happened to you?" he asked, staring at their grimy faces and dirty clothes. "*Who* might have done something to us?"

"Ethan and Mohammed," Josh told him.

Olly ran forward. "And Dad, we've found the Tears!"

Both men stared at her incredulously. Olly held the golden casket out on the palm of her hand and raised the lid. The beautiful sapphires glittered and shined. Jonathan and the professor drew closer, gazing at the jewels.

"What is this, Olivia?" the Professor breathed. "Where did you find these?"

"In the room that devours itself!" Olly replied, grinning.

"Which way did you turn when you went through the secret door?" Josh asked.

"To the right," Jonathan told him.

Olly shrugged. "We went left — and you're not going to believe what we found!"

"But first we have to warn you about Ethan and Mohammed," Josh said.

"*What* about them?" Jonathan asked.

At that moment, Natasha and Audrey Beckmann came running breathlessly into the chamber.

"They're after the Tears of Isis!" Josh said. He glanced at his mother. "Both of them! Ethan was behind the theft of the Elephantine Stone. Mohammed was helping him." He pointed toward the secret door. "They chased us in there. It's a long story, but we managed to get their flashlight and find our way out."

Natasha stared at him in disbelief. "This is insane," she said. "Ethan isn't a *criminal.*"

Jonathan looked hard at Josh. "Are they still down there without any light?" he asked sharply.

"Yes," Olly nodded. "We left them in the Chamber of Light."

Josh opened his mouth to speak, but Jonathan silenced him with a gesture of his hand. He looked at Professor Christie. "We need to get in there and find them," he said.

"Ethan!" Natasha suddenly exclaimed.

Everyone followed the direction of her gaze. She was looking at the secret door and Ethan Cain was there, doubled over, one hand against the wall. His clothes were dirty and torn and there was a raw, bloody graze on his cheek. Blood trailed from the corner of his mouth and his lips were swollen and bruised. "Help me," he panted, almost falling into the room. Jonathan and Natasha ran forward to catch him. He seemed dizzy and breathless. "Mohammed," he murmured. "You have to stop Mohammed before he gets away. He stole the Elephantine Stone!"

"Don't trust him!" Olly shouted. "Mohammed was working for him."

Ethan stared at her in surprise. "That's not true," he protested. "I tried to stop him." He gestured to his face. "He did this to me."

"No," Josh said, glaring at Ethan. "You were working together to steal the Tears of Isis."

Ethan shook his head. He pulled himself upright with a visible effort. "I let Mohammed think I'd help him steal the stone." He looked at Professor Christie. "I thought I could get him to reveal himself if I played along with him," he said. "I was stupid. When I confronted him, he went crazy. I thought he was going to kill me."

"That's not true, Dad," Olly said. "He's lying to you!"

Ethan coughed weakly. "No, Olly, really I'm not," he insisted.

"Then why were you chasing us?" Josh demanded.

"Mohammed was determined to go after you," Ethan said. "I couldn't risk letting him hurt you. So, I went with him."

"That's not how it happened!" Olly exclaimed in exasperation.

Ethan smiled kindly at her. "I don't blame you for being confused, Olly, but I'm telling the truth. There was a long chase through the dark." He glanced up at the professor. "It's immense down there — dozens of rooms and probably miles of corridors. It's a stupendous find!"

"So I've heard," said the professor. "But what about Mohammed?"

Ethan frowned. "Well, we found Olly and Josh in a golden room," he said. "There was a bright light which completely dazzled me. I couldn't see a thing. Then something struck my legs and I stumbled into Mohammed. We both fell. Before either of us could get up, Olly and Josh had taken our flashlight and left. Mohammed was crazy with anger. I could tell he was prepared to hurt Olly and Josh to get the Tears from them. I tried to reason with him, but he attacked me. He had another, smaller flashlight, so he left me there on the floor and went after Olly and Josh. It was a few minutes before I could walk." He shook his head. "I tried to follow him, but I couldn't see which way he had gone. In the end I used my cigar lighter to find my way out." Ethan pulled free from Natasha and Jonathan. "But we must find

Mohammed now," he said anxiously. "There's no time to lose!"

"You're far too badly hurt," Natasha argued. "We need to get you to a doctor."

"You don't actually believe his story, do you?" Olly exclaimed.

Natasha frowned at her. "Stop it, Olly!" she snapped. "Ethan's right — you're just confused." She looked at Josh and her voice softened. "Who wouldn't be after what you've been through? But Ethan got hurt trying to protect you, can't you see that?"

Josh stared speechlessly at his mother.

Olly was lost for words, too. She looked from face to face and realized that no one believed their story. Ethan had won everyone over.

"It doesn't matter," Ethan said, smiling weakly at the two friends. "It was all a misunderstanding." He took a step toward them. "But I have to know one thing: Did you find the Tears of Isis?"

Olly stared at him. He was so persuasive that for a moment she almost believed him. She almost believed that she had conjured up all of the evidence against Ethan in her head. Then she remembered the ferocious look of greed she had seen on his face in the Chamber of Light. However, she knew it was pointless to keep accusing him when everyone else was convinced that she and Josh were just mistaken. Looking coldly into his face, she showed him the golden casket.

Ethan's eyes gleamed as he gazed at the fabulous jewels. "Beautiful," he said. He looked around at the professor. "Congratulations, Professor. There are chambers of treasure back there," he said. "This is the greatest find since Tutankhamen — possibly the greatest untouched hoard ever discovered in Egypt! You're going to be famous."

"That can wait," said Mrs. Beckmann, taking charge of the situation. "First, we need to call the police and tell them about Mohammed. Jonathan — deal with that, please. Natasha and I will take Ethan to my trailer. He can rest there and we'll clean him up and see how much damage has been done." She turned to the youngsters. "Olivia, you can help us. Josh — I'd like you to run over to the diggers' camp. Wake a few of them up and tell them the professor needs them immediately." She looked at the professor. "They can mount an overnight guard on the place, just in case Mohammed is still in the vicinity."

While Olly was still reeling from the turn of events, her father stepped up to her and lifted the casket out of her hands. "These need to be put somewhere safe," he said, closing the lid. "Go with your gran now, Olivia. Tomorrow, we'll study the Tears of Isis to see what secrets they hold."

Olly stared at Josh, stunned by the way the adults had taken over and by how easily Ethan had fooled them all.

Josh gave her a blank, helpless look that showed he was feeling the same way. Then he turned and ran off on the errand that Olly's gran had given him.

~~~

It was a busy night. The police arrived with some bad news of their own. Benjamin Carter was gone — he had bribed a guard and escaped from his cell. A hunt was on, but so far there had been no sign of him.

Police officers examined Mohammed's tent, but found it stripped of his possessions. He had beaten them to it. The laptop — the final shred of evidence that Olly and Josh had hoped might link Ethan Cain to the theft of the Elephantine Stone — was gone.

And the dig supervisor himself seemed to have melted into the desert night. The police promised to do all they could to track him down, but they didn't seem hopeful. One officer stayed at the site to keep watch over the tomb.
~~~

Professor Christie didn't enter the tomb again that night. He spent the evening in his trailer, making calls to Cairo University and the Egyptian authorities, informing them of the find, and inviting them to join him in exploring the extraordinary lost catacombs of Setiankhra's tomb.

It was midnight before the camp began to settle down. Beds were found for Natasha and Ethan. The golden casket that contained the Tears of Isis was locked away in the security box, and Jonathan slept with it by his side.

Neither Josh nor Olly found it easy to sleep. Olly lay wide-eyed far into the night, torn between the almost unbearable excitement of their discovery and her deep dismay that Ethan Cain had fooled everyone. *At least his schemes failed and we beat him to the Tears of Isis*, she told herself. *We have the first Talisman of the Moon*. And comforted by that thought, she eventually drifted into a shallow, restless sleep.

~~~~

It seemed only a few minutes later that Olly was woken by somebody shaking her shoulder. She snuggled deeper under the covers. "Go away, Josh," she mumbled. "You're such a pain!"
~~~~

"Olivia!" It was her gran's voice. "Wake up, now, dear."

Olly forced her eyes open. Audrey Beckmann was leaning over her.

"What time is it?" Olly asked.

"It's still early, but Natasha and Ethan are leaving shortly. I thought you'd want to say good-bye. I've already woken Josh."

Olly was suddenly wide awake. "I thought Ethan was staying till the helicopter was fixed," she said as she hopped out of bed.

"Change of plans," said Gran, picking up her clothes from the floor and handing them to her. "They're both catching a flight from Luxor airport this morning. Apparently there's some kind of problem at Ethan's head office and he has to deal with it personally." She frowned. "How many times have I told you not to throw your things all over the floor when you get undressed?"

Olly was climbing into her clothes. "Sorry, Gran," she said.

Her gran sat down at the end of her bed. "Now, Olly," she began. "I don't want any more nonsense about Ethan." She raised a warning finger. "Make sure you're on your best behavior. And be quick, now." She got up, patted Olly on the back, and left the room.

Olly frowned. Best behavior! If only her gran knew what had *really* happened down in Setiankhra's tomb. But she didn't, and that was that. Olly sighed. At least she and Josh had found the Tears and wrecked Ethan's plans. She'd remember that when she had to wave him good-bye.

Natasha and Ethan were ready to leave by the time Olly appeared. One of the diggers was going to drive them to the airport in the Land Rover. Jonathan, Josh, Audrey Beckmann, and the professor were saying their farewells to the glamorous couple as Olly came up.

"Well, it's been quite a visit, hasn't it?" Natasha said, giving Olly a hug.

Olly smiled. "I'll say." She exchanged a knowing look with Josh.

Ethan turned toward the two friends. "No hard feelings about our little misunderstanding," he said, smiling cheerfully at them. "You should both be very proud," he continued. "You've discovered something that other people have spent entire lifetimes searching for. I only wish I could spare the time to explore the tomb with you."

Olly looked steadily into his eyes and smiled sweetly. "Why do you have to go?" she asked. "Couldn't you stay a little while longer?" She knew the real reason he had changed his plans: Now that the Tears were safely under lock and key, he had no hope of getting his hands on them.

Ethan met her gaze. "Business has to come first," he sighed. He leaned toward her, smiling. "But I'll be following your father's quest for the other Talismans of the Moon with great interest," he told her. "And you never know — I may even find time to visit you now and then and see how you're all doing."

Olly stared at him — for a moment she caught a glint in his eyes that wasn't at all friendly. Then he turned and climbed into the Land Rover with a final wave.

The little group watched and waved as the Land Rover headed down toward the river.

"Did you see that look he gave me?" Olly whispered to Josh.

"Yes," Josh whispered back. "And I didn't like that comment about watching your father's search for the other Talismans with 'great interest'!"

"Me neither," Olly agreed. "I'm sure we haven't

seen the last of him. But we beat him this time, and if he comes back for more, we'll just have to beat him again."

"What are you two whispering about?" Mrs. Beckmann asked.

"Nothing, Gran," Olly replied lightly. "When's breakfast?"

~~~~

It was shortly after breakfast that the first of the visitors arrived on site. Professor Khalil Fehr, Head of Egyptology at Cairo University, was a tall, courteous man with gray hair and a face as dark and wrinkled as a walnut. He brought with him a team of archaeologists and scientists who had flown in to examine the great discoveries. Professor Christie was in his element among so many experts on ancient Egypt. Soon he was lost in conversation and debate with his eminent colleagues.

Olly was desperate to go down into the tomb again. She couldn't understand why it was taking so long for her father to get around to it.

"A lot of important people need to be involved," her gran explained. "We're visitors in this country, Olivia, remember that. Your father wants to do this right."

Over the next hour, various Egyptian dignitaries
~~~~

and government officials began to arrive from Luxor, Aswan, and Cairo. They greeted Professor Christie enthusiastically, congratulating him on his find, all of them eager to see the ancient treasures that had been discovered.

"It's not me you have to thank," the professor told them all modestly. "My daughter, Olivia, and her friend Josh made the most astonishing finds."

At last, everyone gathered around the hole through which Olly and Josh had escaped the tomb the previous night. Jonathan had been up since shortly after dawn, supervising a team of diggers who had worked to make the hole safe. The roof was now shored up with timbers, and more steps had been added to make the descent into the chamber easier.

"This is not the method by which we first entered the tomb," the professor explained. "But the other route is much more difficult and dangerous."

"I'll say," muttered Olly, thinking of the shattered skeletons beneath the bridge.

"Shh!" hissed Josh. "He's talking about us!"

"My daughter, Olivia, and my assistant's brother, Josh, are the ones who actually found the Chamber of Light and the Tears of Isis," the professor was saying.

All eyes turned to the two friends. Olly grinned and seemed to glow with pride, while Josh, embarrassed by so much attention, endeavored to hide behind his shaggy blond hair.

"We will now enter the tomb of Setiankhra," Professor Christie continued. "And I would like Olly and Josh to be our guides."

Olly and Josh stared at each other in astonishment. Neither of them had expected this.

"You're the only ones who know the way," Jonathan pointed out to them quietly, smiling at their shocked expressions.

The friends soon recovered from their surprise, and side by side they led the way down into the catacombs of Setiankhra's tomb.

As they made their way through the spectacular hall of treasures, they heard gasps of amazement from the group behind them. Josh looked at Olly and grinned.

"I can see that being heroic explorers is going to take up an awful lot of our time," Olly said to him thoughtfully.

Josh nodded. "You're right. I mean we still have all the other Talismans of the Moon to find for a start. Then we'll have to figure out how they reveal the Archives. I don't know when we'll be able to fit in schoolwork."

A determined look crossed Olly's face. "I don't think eminent explorers should have to do schoolwork anyway," she said firmly.

Josh laughed. "I can't wait to hear it when you attempt to convince your gran," he told her.

They had reached the golden doors at the heart of the hall of treasures. Here they stopped and turned to the party of archaeologists. "Ladies and gentlemen," Olly announced. "Welcome to the Chamber of Light!"

And as she and Josh opened the doors, the crowd of scholars waited in silent anticipation to share the friends' brilliant discovery.

Take a sneak peek at the next

CHRONICLES OF THE MOON

LEGEND OF THE LOST CITY

The Myth of Chang-O

In ancient days in China, it was said that ten suns lived in the giant Lau Shang tree that grew in the Heavenly Lands beyond the Eastern Horizon. These ten suns were the offspring of the Sky God Di Jun and the Goddess Xi He. Their mother decreed that only one sun should burn in the sky at a time, and she decided the order in which her sons would cross the heavens, each taking their turn in Di Jun's chariot. But the unruly suns became discontented with discipline their mother's and they came up with a plan to break free of their tedious duties.

One morning, all ten suns appeared together, blazing defiantly in the sky. They ignored their mother when she called for them to return to the tree. They did not even heed the mighty voice of Di Jun, their heavenly father. They were free at last, and they were determined to remain so.

At first, the people of Earth greeted the ten suns with delight, but soon their crops began to wither under the fierce heat, their rivers dried up, and their lands became parched. The Emperor of China implored Di Jun to help the people and to restore the old order of one sun a day.

Di Jun sent messengers to Earth: a mighty archer named Hou-Yi and his beautiful wife, Chang-O. Di Jun gave Hou-Yi a red bow and a quiver full of white arrows. He hoped that the arrows would help Hou-Yi frighten the ten rebellious suns back to their duties. But when Hou-Yi saw the scorched and thirsty earth, he grew angry and, one by one, he shot down nine of the suns from the sky.

The people were delighted and proclaimed Hou-Yi a hero, but Di Jun was angry at the deaths of his sons, and he condemned Hou-Yi and Chang-O to remain on Earth and become mortal.

But Hou-Yi refused to be mortal. He went into the Uttermost West and sought the help of the Queen Goddess. She gave him a pill of everlasting life and told him to prepare himself with twelve months of prayer and fasting before taking the pill.

After returning to his home, Hou-Yi hid the pill and began his long preparations. One night, his wife,

Chang-O, was awoken by the delightful fragrance of flowers. She rose and noticed a single white moonbeam, and she followed it to find that is was shining from the pill. Chang-O picked up the pill and swallowed it — and found that she could fly.

She flew through the house and out into the lotus-scented garden, singing joyfully as she soared beneath the full moon. Her husband awoke and, when he realized what Chang-O had done, he became terribly angry. Chang-O fled her husband's wrath, but he pursued her over mountains and plains, through bamboo forests, and across great rivers, until, in her fear, she flew up to the moon seeking refuge.

Her only companion on the moon was a magical hare that pounded medicinal herbs with a mortar and pestle. Regretting her actions and seeking to appease her husband, Chang-O coughed up half the pill. She then commanded the hare to pound up the half-pill and make of a new pill that she could take back to Hou-Yi.

Each year in China, at the Festival of the Moon, the people eat mooncakes to symbolize the pill made by the hare and to honor the Moon Goddess, Chang-O.

~~~~~

Olivia Christie stopped reading the legend and looked up from the book, her blue eyes shining. "Well," she said, "what do you think of that?"
~~~~~

Josh Welles smiled. "Nice story, Olly," he replied, glancing up from his laptop computer. "So what happened? Did Chang-O find Hou-Yi? Did he ever become immortal again?"

"I don't know," Olly said. "I haven't read that far. But I will."

Twelve-year-old Olly and her best friend, Josh, were seated side by side in a large passenger airplane. Olly had been reading aloud the story of Chang-O, the Chinese Moon Goddess, as preparation for their trip. Josh's eyes were trained on his laptop, which showed a map of Asia. A red line indicated their flight path. Their party had boarded a plane at London Heathrow before dawn that morning. A quick transfer in Paris, just as the sun was rising, had brought them aboard their present aircraft for the ten-hour flight to Beijing, China.

While they were halfway to the Chinese capital, that was not their final destination. Their trip would include two more plane rides, the first stop being in the Sichuan Province at the ancient city of Chengdu. From there, the party would begin the final leg of their extensive journey to the ancient ruins that had recently been revealed along the banks of the mighty Minjiang River.

Olly's father was the renowned archaeologist Professor Kenneth Christie. The Chinese authorities had requested his presence at this historic dig, and Olly was traveling with him. Her mother had died two years ago, and, since then, Olly had frequently accompanied her father on his international expeditions, where she was looked after and tutored by her grandmother, Audrey Beckmann. Olly — short for Olivia — loved traveling with her dad. The exploration and archaelogical digs were a good match for her adventurous nature, much better than staying home in England. She especially liked trips like this one, where they would be seeing part of an ancient world that had been lost for centuries. The old secrets and stories — like the Myth of Chang-O — fascinated her. Besides, she had a very personal reason to be interested in things like curses and myths.

Professor Christie's assistant, a talented archaeological student named Jonathan Welles, was Josh's twenty-four-year-old brother. Their mother was the famous movie actress, Natasha Welles. Because her career did not provide Josh with a very stable home life, it had been arranged that he should accompany his brother and the Christies on their continent-hopping adventures. This arrangement worked out well, because he and Olly had soon become the best of friends.

Audrey Beckmann was more than happy to tutor Josh as well. In fact, Audrey willingly voiced rather often that she was relieved to have Josh around since he was far more reliable and practical than her headstrong granddaughter.

Olly peered out of the small porthole. The airplane hung in a clear blue sky above an endless panorama of barren, snowcapped mountains. As she stared down at the breathtaking but forbidding wildlands of the Alatau Mountains, Olly felt the wonderful knot of excitement in her stomach that always accompanied the start of a new quest.

It was only a few weeks ago that they had been in the Valley of the Kings in Egypt, excavating the ancient tomb of Pharaoh Setiankhra. Olly almost couldn't believe that she and Josh had actually been the ones to find the golden room deep under the cliffs — the room known as the Chamber of Light. In spite of ancient booby traps and deadly rock slides, the two friends had escaped the tomb with the two sapphires that were known as the Tears of Isis. And, according to legend, the Tears of Isis was one of the priceless Talismans of the Moon.

If the legends were true, then the Talismans of the Moon were created thousands of years ago by the moon-priests of ancient civilizations in different parts of the world. Each culture made its own talisman, and it was said that if they were all brought together at the right time and place, then great wonders would be revealed. Together, the talismans could answer age-old secrets.

In the course of his recent archaeological investigations, Professor Christie had found evidence that the talismans might be more than mere legend. Ever since then, he had been determined to track them all down and unlock their secrets.

Olly breathed a sigh of pure joy and settled back in her seat, thrilled to be on a new adventure.

Follow Olly and Josh's
quest for the second talisman,
the Mooncake of Chang-O, in the

LEGEND OF THE LOST CITY